AMONG THESE BONES
Book 1

AMANDA LUZZADER

KNOWLEDGE FOREST
PRESS

To my children, Hudson and Dawson,
from whom I have learned the most about love

CHAPTER 1

We sat on our bikes in the empty street, my grown-up son and I. The son I didn't remember, the son I would forget again. We sat on our bikes, watching the house.

It was an ordinary house, but nobody was home, and nobody had been for a long time. The windows were broken. A mailbox lay pushed over and crumpled. Chains hung from the swing set, whining as they swung in the breeze. One house on a street of such houses. One street in a neighborhood of such streets.

"That one?" I asked.

Arie unfolded his smudged and rumpled map of the neighborhood, where the progress of our searches was marked in pencil. He nodded, and so I tightened my ponytail. We rolled our bikes into the thicket of weeds where a lawn had once grown. It'd been hard to find a bike tall enough for Arie and almost as hard to find one that wasn't too tall for me. We climbed the steps to the porch. The storm door had been ripped from its hinges, and the door frame was cracked, probably from a search a long time ago, but maybe something worse. Arie pushed on the door and it swung open.

We stayed for a moment on the porch.

"Careful," I said.

"Mom," he said.

At the beginning of the year, I'd told him he didn't have to call me "mom". He could call me Alison, like everyone else, but he called me mom anyway. And I liked it.

"I don't want to be here in the first place," I said. "Just—be careful."

We never knew what we'd find beyond the closed doors. Booby traps, wild animals, mummified corpses. And that was assuming the house was unoccupied. There could be Agency goons inside looking to make trouble, or other lawless characters.

I was there to make sure Arie stayed safe. Something about the houses compelled him to search them, and he'd search whether or not I came along. So, I helped him. I was his mother.

Arie stepped in first, like always. He stood in the living room a few seconds, then shoved his hands in his pockets and took a long, slow look around. He was thin, and tall enough that his head almost touched the ceiling fan. I might never remember how he grew from baby to kid to teen and then into this tall young man.

He glanced at me over his shoulder. "You coming?"

Even with my shoes on, I felt the crusted dust on the floor as it crunched underfoot. The odors of abandonment, of decay. How many years had passed since someone had stood in that place?

There was always a certain excitement when we searched the houses, but I also felt a sense of not belonging. Like the home itself was waiting vainly for the children to start up a Nerf war in the basement, waiting for the husband to steal a kiss from his wife in the kitchen. When we entered there was disappointment in the air. We were the wrong family in the wrong home.

Arie went to a stack of magazines on a side table in

the corner. He held them up with both hands and blew the dust into a gray cloud that lingered.

"I think I'll be a while," he said, taking a seat on the deflated, filthy sofa.

"Don't take forever," I said. The longer we were outside of our Zone the more dangerous it was, but Arie was already thumbing through the dust-caked magazines, examining each of the covers.

"Seen it," he said, tossing the first one aside. "Seen it. Seen it." He tossed them away. The next one he opened.

I wandered into the kitchen. Most of the cabinets gaped open, the doors broken and hanging. Nothing in them but crumbs and cobwebs, anyway. The food was all gone. Had been for years. Medicine, too, and most other useful things. That wasn't why we were there.

On the dining room table there sat a tea set painted with roses. Kettle, teacup, saucer. I took a seat at the table and looked into the cup. Inside there was a succession of brown lines where the tea had once been but had dried away. The teaspoon had been set on the saucer as though its owner had risen from the table expecting to return after only a moment.

Arie rummaged in the living room and then continued down a hall to the other rooms on the ground floor. Next, I heard him bumping around and sorting in the back of the house.

I looked back at the tea set. Someone had made tea and it had remained there—undisturbed, evaporating. I wondered about the others just as much as I wondered about Arie and myself. What had really happened to them?

Arie poked his head into the kitchen and ran a hand through his hair to sweep the long bangs from his eyes.

"I'm going up," he said. He shoved a few magazines and what appeared to be a photo album into his backpack, then headed for the staircase.

As I rose to follow him, I put the teacup and spoon into the pocket of my coat.

The curtains were drawn shut in the first bedroom upstairs, making it nearly too dark to see. Arie split them wide open and sunlight poured in. He stared out the window. I joined him.

"Hey," I said, pointing, "a Ferris wheel."

Out beyond the trees and shingled rooftops, the skeletal wheel with its spokes rose lonely and still on the horizon.

"Yeah," said Arie.

"I never noticed it," I said.

"You've never been this far south."

"It's getting late," I said. "You about finished here?"

Arie stood there awhile, concentrating on the distant Ferris wheel, as though he might remember.

"Arie."

He turned away from the window and said, "I'll search this one if you'll do the one down the hall."

"Okay," I said. "Let's make it fast. I want to get out of here."

"Look everywhere," he reminded me as I went. "Not just the drawers and shelves. Under stuff, behind."

"I know, I know," I said. "People hide things. Don't be so bossy."

He smiled sheepishly. "Sorry."

The room had been a girl's bedroom. A teenager. A four-poster princess bed sat ruined in the center of the room beneath the shroud of a faded canopy. Curled and faded posters clung to the walls. The makeup table and dresser had been ransacked. I stepped inside and knelt in the debris of school supplies and clothing.

I pawed through a pile of textbooks. Western Civ, Algebra II—useless. There was a spiral notebook the girl had kept for biology class—not enough blank pages to keep. There were dingy stuffed animals and once-pretty blouses and a curling iron. Nothing of any use. Arie was so much better at this. I lifted the dust-caked mattress, looked under the bed. Nothing.

I'd had a room like that once. I assumed so, anyway. It was only common sense. Before all of the trouble, long ago, I'd been a teenage girl, somewhere. Maybe someday I'd remember.

In the corner of the room there was a bookshelf. Most of its contents lay toppled out and scattered. Books about teen lovers and winsome horses and young wizards. Arie never wanted any of those. The shelf was heavy and tall. At the top, where the top of the bookcase almost touched the ceiling, there was a dark line of shadow.

It was a hiding place. I stood up.

"Mom," Arie called from the other room.

"Just a second," I said.

"No. Now. Quick!"

I heard the engine rumbling as I went down the hall to the other bedroom where Arie crouched at the window. He made a frantic gesture to stop me. I dropped to all fours and crawled to the window. We peeked over the sill.

An armored troop carrier turned the corner at the top of the block and rolled down the street. Enormous, angular, with a machine gun protruding from a turret that traversed slowly, seeking.

"Patrol," I said.

"They'll see our bikes."

It wasn't against the rules for us to be here. Not officially. But that wouldn't matter to an Agency goon bent on mayhem.

I put my hand on Arie's arm to steady him, and then chanced a glance down into the yard, where our bikes lay in the tall weeds.

"We need to get downstairs," I said. "We could get stuck up here."

Arie slung his backpack and we crawled from the room through the drifts of dust on the carpet. The noise of the vehicle grew louder. We picked our way down the stairs, ducking to see out of the windows of the ground floor. We'd seen a few patrols before, but never this close, and never so far from our Zone.

"Are they stopping here?" Arie hissed. "I think they're stopping."

"Arie," I snapped, "quit freaking out. Jesus. Just wait."

"What if they catch us?"

I shushed him furiously. "Hold still."

There were stories of what they'd do to us. We knew people who'd disappeared, and we'd even seen a few beatings and arrests with our own eyes. And that was inside the Zone boundaries.

The troop carrier slowed as it approached the house where we hid. Then it stopped. The hatch on the turret swung open and a soldier appeared. I suddenly knew Arie was about to bolt. Something about the way his backed tensed—technically, I barely knew this boy, but I knew for sure he was getting ready to run. I put my hand on his shoulder and squeezed hard.

"Hold still."

The soldier hopped down from the fender of the troop carrier and walked to the side of the road. He looked in either direction as he unfastened his pants, and then he relieved himself. Our bikes lay in the weeds near enough that he could have sprayed them if he'd known they were there.

After a minute he fastened his pants, mounted the troop carrier, and slid down into the turret. The hatch swung closed with a thunk, and the vehicle rolled on until it was out of sight.

"He's gone," I breathed. "Time to get home."

We waited in the living room for a few minutes to see if the patrol would return or if another would come along, but the street remained quiet and empty. My hands were shaking as we crept down into the living room. Arie opened the front door an inch or two and looked through the crack.

Then I remembered.

"Wait," I said. "I nearly forgot. Wait here a sec."

I took the stairs a couple at a time, raising clouds of gray dust. There were few windows upstairs, and it had gotten darker. I felt my way to the girl's bedroom and found the tall bookshelf. I got on my tiptoes and felt along the top. There was something there. My fingers touched it. A box maybe, or a book. The shelf stood too high for me grasp whatever hid there. I stretched and reached and nearly pulled the shelf over on top of me, but then I had it.

A diary.

Arie waited at the bottom of the stairs. As I came down, I held out the diary. When he saw it, his mouth opened a bit, but he didn't snatch it away from me or tear it open. He took it carefully, with both hands. Then he ran his fingers over the cover, which was a collage of flowered stickers and decals. He smiled a little.

"Good job, Mom," he said opening the diary.

I knew that Arie was my son only because they'd told me so. I'd known for less than a year, and in three more months, they'd need to tell me again. We both had blue eyes and dark hair, but I didn't remember feeding him or teaching him to ride a bike. However, as we left the Agency facility that morning nine months before, I knew I was his mother. When he coiled up on the stairs, ready to run, I knew. And when he turned to the first handwritten page of the flowered diary, I knew again. My son was happy. I'd made him happy. Even with how much it scared me to be caught out there in those desolate suburbs, it was worth it to see him smile.

"Read later," I said. "We gotta go."

"'Kay." He snapped it shut.

We climbed down the front steps and waded through the weeds to our bikes.

"Where'd you find it?" he asked.

"On top of the bookshelf in this little crack way up— did you hear that?"

"Hear what."

Something was moving through the backyard. I heard the rustling of dead weeds, and when I turned to see, I caught a glimpse of motion.

"Get down," I snapped at Arie.

We crouched.

"They must have seen us and circled back on foot," I whispered.

Fast movement to our left and to our right. Then, behind us, too. It wasn't the patrol.

"Dogs," I shouted. "Run!"

CHAPTER 2

They burst from the overgrown brush at the side of the house. Three or four of them—snarling and barking. They barreled after us as we sprinted across the yard. Arie was a lot faster than me.

"Tree," shouted Arie.

A fruit tree stood nearly leafless at the edge of the yard. Arie made it there first. He was taller than me by a head. He grabbed a branch seven or eight feet up, and he walked his legs up the trunk until he was perched like some enormous chimp. I ran as fast as I could, crashing through the weed stalks dry with autumn, the dogs so close behind I heard their hoarse panting and the popping sound their jaws made as they snapped at me.

Stretched out on the high branch, Arie extended his arm. I took hold, but as Arie swung me up, one of the dogs caught my pant leg. He was big and black. With a thrash of his head he tore me from Arie's grip, and I tumbled back into the weeds.

"Mom!" Arie yelled. He jumped down.

The black dog clamped onto my leg, shaking his head and tugging at me. I felt his teeth tear open the skin of my ankle. A smaller dog bit the sleeve of my coat and pulled me in the other direction. The third dog loped in, snarling and nipping at me. I swung at them, kicked at them, drowning in a sea of hot savagery.

Arie got my sleeve free but then the two smaller dogs went after him. He raced around the weedy yard in a crazed game of tag, spinning and dodging as they snapped at him.

I kicked the black dog, connecting with his cheeks and snout, but he only flinched and bit harder. His body shuddered with guttural growls. The whites of his eyes showed when he shook me. I thought he might rip my leg off at the knee.

More dogs came galloping into the yard. Arie tripped and stumbled and was buried in a frenzy of fur and bared fangs. So many dogs. Beneath their snarling, I heard Arie shouting. The black dog let go of my leg and lunged for my throat, head low, ears flattened. I shoved him away and tried to rise, but his big paws were on my stomach, my ribcage, pressing me down. He forced his muzzle between my arms and hands, teeth bared. For a split second our eyes locked. His mouth opened.

There came a deafening boom.

The black dog convulsed and then went limp. I raised my head. The other dogs stood frozen, looking toward the street. Another boom, a gunshot. The dogs flinched in unison. A few scampered away, tails tucked. I rolled to one side and the black dog slid off me and lay still.

I stood. My pant leg was torn and bloody, and my leg burned. Arie kicked at the dogs as the last of them ran yapping down the street. Their claws clicked dryly on the pavement.

Standing in the street was a stout woman holding a pistol. She wiped her nose with the back of her sleeve.

"You kids all right?"

We checked ourselves, turning and twisting. Arie's hand dripped blood. My leg began to throb miserably.

We were covered in dry leaves, dead flower petals, and the broken stems of thistles.

"We'll live," I said, brushing the weedy debris from my clothes.

Arie went to the sidewalk and picked up his backpack. The magazines and books he'd found had spilled and lay fanned out on the concrete. He collected them and returned them to the pack while the woman watched.

"What's all 'at?" she asked.

"Nothing," said Arie. "My stuff."

"You shouldn't be out here," she scolded. Her voice was loud and brassy. "But if you're gonna be, you oughta least be able to defend yourself."

The woman brandished the pistol and then put it away somewhere under her coat. When she ambled closer, she limped, favoring her left leg. Her face was lumpy and her hair was cropped short like a man's. With the toe of her boot, she nudged the black dog's body. It made no movement.

"Look at this," she said, pointing to the dog's collar with a stubby, grimy finger. The collar was sun-faded and frowzy. "This was somebody's pet."

I noticed the dog's ribs and the thinness of its body. The woman bent down and tilted her head back to read the tarnished metal tag through her battered bifocals.

"Chieftain," she said, frowning. "His name. This is what happens when living things get forgot. They turn mean. Some of these others might have been littered since Year One. But not this guy. He was part of somebody's family. Back before."

She patted him on the neck, then pushed her glasses higher up her round, pitted nose. She squinted at me.

My ears still rang from the gunshot, and I struggled

11

to catch my breath. "Thank you," I panted.

"This makes me really mad," she said. "I love dogs. I'm an animal lover." She jabbed her finger at me. "You owe me now. Big time."

"What do you want? Food? We have a little food. Some good firewood, too," I said.

"We'll figure it out another day," she said. Then she pointed to my leg. "You're gonna need stitches."

Arie was clutching his hand to his chest. Blood ran down his forearm and dripped from his elbow.

"You, too," she said to him. "That looks bad."

Arie nodded.

"What's your names?" she asked. We told her.

She jerked her chin at Arie's backpack. "Ya like books, huh?"

Arie didn't answer.

"Guess you was real lucky I come round when I did," she said. Then she shrugged and waddled off the way she came.

"Hey, wait," I said. "Who are you?"

She didn't look back. Over her shoulder she yelled, "Ruby," and kept going.

*

I hadn't been to the infirmary since the beginning of the year, and if there had been any way to avoid it, I wouldn't have gone back. We knew of people who went there for a minor illness or injury but never came back out. A very nice man who'd lived across the street from us was taken into custody for misconduct and then never heard from more. We knew we had to go back at the new year to take the serum, but we'd only do that because we'd been told we would die if we didn't, and the only reason we believed it was that we had no one else to listen to.

Cuts and bruises we could deal with on our own. But, as always, there was disease to consider. Infection, rabies—and worse. The meat of Arie's palm was punctured and deeply lacerated. He'd wrapped it with a clean cloth when we got home, and I'd splashed it with iodine, but we couldn't seem to completely stop the bleeding. It oozed continuously. There were ragged bite marks and a long gash on my calf, already surrounded by purple bruising. The pain radiated up into my hip and waist. Riding my bike to the Agency infirmary was agony.

We stopped the bikes on a wide empty street leading to the massive but spartan cinder block building. I traded a long look with Arie.

He shook his head slowly.

"We have to," I said, nodding at his arm.

After chaining the bikes to a dilapidated chain link fence, we went on. The entrance lay on the far side of an empty courtyard of crumbling asphalt. Barring the entrance there stood a low wall of concrete Jersey barriers and a squad of uniformed goons. Those we called goons weren't actual Agency personnel, but they carried batons and wore sidearms on their hips.

When Arie and I were halfway across the courtyard, one of the goons stopped us with his outstretched palm.

"Stop there," he shouted. "Turn around, put your hands on top of your head, kneel down, and cross your ankles."

We did so. The pain in my leg made me lightheaded as I knelt, but of course we had to do as they said. My skin went clammy. Arie was breathing rapidly, and his eyes darted frantically.

I turned to him and said, "Take it easy."

"No talking," shouted the goon. "Sit tight there. Don't move."

My knees throbbed. After what felt like ages, I heard the crunching footsteps of two goons approaching from behind. I could not see them but I knew that one trained a gun on us while the other held an electronic ID chip scanner.

"Don't move," one of the goons repeated as he stood over me.

I held my breath. He passed the chip scanner over the back of my neck where my ID chip was embedded, and there was a beep.

"What happened?" said the goon.

"Dogs," I said. "Dogs attacked us."

"Get up," he said.

They ushered us through the courtyard, and we were admitted through a series of air washes and tightly sealed doors. I limped along. Agency personnel eyed us from behind layers of Lexan as we moved through the gauntlet. Our ID chips were scanned a few times more, and at last we were shown to an examination room. There we were joined by a technician in a tight-fitting, plastic-skinned hermetic suit.

He was afraid of us. Through the clear face screen of the h-suit, we could plainly see he was nervous. Perhaps he was new. All that blood. His hands trembled as he swabbed the blood and dirt from Arie's palm.

Arie winced as the technician turned his hand over to close the cuts with stitches.

"I'm gonna need you to hold really still," snapped the technician. His voice was buzzy through the mask. "This needle is very sharp."

Soon the technician was joined by another man in an identical h-suit. He had a pen and clipboard.

"And where did you say you were when this happened?" he buzzed at me.

"By our house," I answered. "A bunch of dogs came from out of nowhere."

He turned to Arie. "Is that what happened?"

Arie nodded.

"Please," the technician pleaded coldly, holding the needle away from Arie's wound, "quit moving, or I'll go and get someone to hold you down." A fog had formed at his mouth on the clear face screen. Only his eyes were visible. He glared at Arie a moment. Arie nodded and was still, and the technician returned to his work.

It felt odd to be considered a threat, but I understood. Because we'd almost died. I don't mean me and Arie in the neighborhoods, attacked by dogs. I mean all of us. The entire human race, so they said. It was hard to wrap my mind around it, to even consider that humans almost didn't exist anymore. But that's what we were told—that it was a pandemic, that the world's population shrank by an unthinkable eighty percent.

Of course, I didn't remember any of that. No one did. Because the serum that saved us also wiped away our memories.

Everyone had received the first dose. Everyone still alive when the Agency released the serum, I mean. Infected or uninfected—everyone got the shot and everyone forgot.

That was Year One.

This was all explained to us at an orientation the day after we awoke from the serum treatment, about nine months previously. I was there with a class of sixty or so others. We were all dazed, and some didn't seem to be paying attention at all, but I wasn't alone in finding it all impossible to believe. An entire civilization with no memories. How did we survive?

I raised my hand and asked that question.

"There are few records from that period," answered the Agency woman from behind the face screen of her suit. "We can only imagine that it was very difficult," she added mechanically. "We are very fortunate."

After Year One, only those who were infected got the shot each year, and that included Arie and me. The shot saved us, supposedly kept the virus down. But we forgot everything with every shot, and every year we got the shot again. The Agency was there to remind us who we were, who we had been.

I shouldn't say we forgot everything. Some memories stayed no matter what. I knew how to talk and walk and eat. And there weren't many cars around, but I knew I could drive one if I ever had the chance—I even knew somehow that I could drive a manual transmission.

"Procedural memory" it's called, the things you can do without thinking about them. I could read and write just fine. Do math.

We retained what are termed "implicit memories," too. I knew what roses, elephants, and ice cream cones were, even if I didn't remember ever having seen one. And that's the main thing we were missing: explicit memories. Context, events, identities. I knew what an amusement park was, but could not place myself ever visiting one. And our identities—all gone. The Agency had to tell us each year who we were and where we belonged. Worse than that, we started over every year, and we depended on them and had to trust them. It was like waking up in a different place than where you went to bed, only to be told by some stranger that the person who fell asleep no longer existed, and that it was your job to take her place.

"Maybe we'll remember next year."

That's what we said. We sometimes said it as often

as "God bless you" or even "hello." Maybe we'll remember next year. Agency scientists, it was said, were constantly working on the serum's formula—desperate to remove the side effect—but how could they be expected to work in our best interest? They didn't know us. No one knew anyone. How could they possibly be more worried about us than themselves? Who could blame them for staying behind their glass walls and hermetic suits? We had nothing to offer them, nothing to offer anyone, and only a dim and blunted hope that we might survive to see some kind of improvement.

We had become a race of phantoms.

CHAPTER 3

The man at the turnstile held out his hand.

He didn't smile or nod. He just put out his open hand as though I might or might not give him something, but he didn't really care either way. In my hand there was a ticket of some kind, so I stepped forward and gave him that. He took it and then retrieved a strip of brightly colored plastic from somewhere. He held it up. I stood looking at him.

"Wanna gimme your wrist?" he asked.

I raised my arm and with a quick motion he wrapped the band around my wrist and fastened it.

"Have fun," he said.

The turnstile clunked as I pushed it and then I was through. The sun was going down but there were hundreds of electric bulbs strobing in the late-summer auburn light. Somewhere a calliope played a marching tune, and there was an aroma of popcorn.

I saw a ride with arms like an octopus which rotated slowly at first and then faster and then inclined until it was almost upright. There was another ride with a long fiberglass pirate ship that swung like a woozy pendulum, higher and higher, until the passengers began to squeal.

People milled in every direction beneath the galaxy of winking lights. Some of the people wandered unhurried, and others ran from place to place. I saw a young couple in a strolling embrace. Mothers with children in tow. I came to the tilt-o-whirl and in the gaps between the spinning riders I saw the blur of the faces on the opposite side, rushing past like memories of people I once knew.

I turned a corner as though I knew where I was headed and saw the ring-toss and milk-can games with their candy-striped awnings. The carnies leaned into the midway, cajoling. I ignored them and came to an open place where the tallest ride of them all rose shimmering like an immense and gaudy clock against the blushing sky.

The Ferris wheel.

Along the concrete entrance platform, the line of waiting revelers extended and folded back on itself and then folded again. I stood in the line shuffling forward and watching the wheel turn. There were arrays of incandescent lights and tubes of neon along its great spokes and their sequenced flashing created patterns like spirals and the waves made by a pebble dropped in a pool.

I reached the head of the line. A girl wearing cargo shorts and a visor waved me forward and I was seated in the gondola hanging from the bottom of the ride. The girl clamped the safety bar across the bench and then stepped on a pedal in the concrete floor of the platform.

"Keep your hands inside the ride at all times," she said without inflection. "Have fun."

The gondola surged backward and up so that another gondola could be emptied of its passengers and reloaded. I moved backward and up. Each time the gondola swayed gently. Backward and up.

Soon I was at the top of the wheel and I could see

the park glistening like an electric birthday cake. I saw the town beyond, too. There were street lamps and window lights and the headlamps of cars moving in the streets, sights not seen in the dead and dark streets of the Zones.

There were those who believed we still had memories, that they hadn't been erased but were locked in the recesses of our minds, the key hidden but waiting, maybe even hoping to be found. That's what Arie believed. And me, too. So, it's no wonder we were fascinated by our own dreams. We wondered constantly whether the places and people we dreamed of were somehow significant.

Or real.

The gondola came over the top of the wheel, plunged down into the noisy park, swept backward over the platform, and ascended again. The girl in the visor worked some lever on a control board and the ride went a little faster.

As I came over the top again, I turned my head, and seated with me in the gondola there was a boy of eight or nine years old.

Did our night minds awaken at sundown and go to work in the dark, reordering puzzle pieces in hopes of someday re-assembling our lives? That was the question: whether our dreams were encoded messages to decipher. Or were they only random images—the arbitrary firing of synapses without meaning?

In some ways, it didn't matter. Because in either case, the dreams at least revealed places and faces we couldn't recall before, and there was hope in that. And so we longed for dreams, for the hope of them. Hope was precious.

That's why I watched the boy as the ride spun faster.

He knew who I was. He grinned at me. Then he gripped the safety bar and we both watched the ground rush up at us as we fell to earth. Then backward and up again.

The wheel spun faster. Like a bicycle tire, like a fan. Everything was a blur, sickening. The carnival lights glared hotly. As the gondola arced over the top again and again, the ground rose and fell around me like the distressed breathing of a puppy or a baby.

And when I looked across the bench of the gondola again, the boy was gone. In his place sat a man who laughed as he looked at me with the lights reflected dazzlingly in his eyes

I always tried to write my dreams down. Always. But it was difficult. In that hazy space where the twin hemispheres of dream world and real world melted together, I often couldn't tell fantasy from reality. Like the boy in the gondola. I knew who he was. Who he must be. Of course I knew. But holding on to the images in the dreams, especially the people, was like clutching handfuls of sand. The more tightly I held it, the quicker it leaked from my fingers. In the dreams I could see them clearly. The boy, the man. The lines and contours of their faces were familiar. But sometimes, before I could awake and find my journal and pen, the only thing that remained in my mind was the certainty that I'd dreamed something, somebody. Even now, as I wondered what it might take to rise and light a candle and grope around for my writing supplies, there was a blaze of light and thundering of footsteps in the hallway that wrenched me from my sleep.

*

"Power's on! Power's on!" Arie shouted, pounding on the wall as he stamped down the hallway.

I propped myself on my elbows and squinted at the

electric light. We always left all the light switches on so that we'd know. The power might come on every day for a week, or it might not come on at all for a month. And it might stay on for a couple hours, or a whole day, or it might be just a few minutes. I rolled out of bed and followed Arie. By the time I reached him, he was tapping the side of the television impatiently, waiting for his devices to start up.

The television blinked on and displayed the input menu. Arie had cobbled together an assortment of video players and computers—devices to read virtually any data storage media in existence. He even had a VCR for the old tapes we sometimes found. Everything was connected by a tangle of cables and adapters decipherable only to Arie. He checked the connections, pressed a few buttons, and loaded a disc.

On the screen, a roomful of children with party hats appeared. I stared at the scene, at the children. The image bobbed and panned. The children laughed. A parent waved at the camera. Zoom in on the gifts stacked in front of a grinning, dark-eyed boy. He looked so happy. He had waited all year for this. Zoom out.

Arie shook his head and pressed the fast-forward button. The party continued in fast motion. Wrapping paper vanished from the gifts to reveal toys, a sweater, a basketball. A cake appeared, its candles pulsing manically. Arie pressed the button again and it went faster. The camera panned crazily as the children sang. Then the candles were extinguished and the cake was obliterated in an eye blink. A party game commenced and was concluded in a few seconds. A few seconds more and the room was empty but for a few adults, and the video was over.

Arie pressed eject button, grabbed the disc, and

tossed it over his shoulder.

"Mom!" he shouted. "Get the scanners going!" He grabbed another disc from the side table, where there was a foot-high stack of discs and a litter of memory cards from cameras and phones. He set the new disc on the ejected tray, which whined in protest as he crammed it back in.

I shuffled to the stack of police scanners which sat atop the unused refrigerator, turned them on, and set each to scan. The scanners beeped a few times and then the lights began to strobe in sequence, cycling from frequency to frequency, searching. One had green lights and another amber and on the top unit they were red. When they were all blinking, the effect was that of a tiny amusement park.

Next, I switched on a portable multi-band radio and held the speaker to my ear. I turned the tuning dial, drifting slowly through all the FM stations, listening. When the green plastic indicator needle slid to the end of the band, I switched to AM and rotated the dial in the opposite direction. Next was UHF, then the weather band, and there were others. The radio was probably manufactured in the 1960s, but Arie said it had a very high-quality amplifier and could pick up the full spectrum of commercial broadcasts—had there been any. There were terminals on the back of the radio and to these Arie had attached a length of flat wire that ran to antennas on the roof. With my ear touching the speaker, I moved the dial as slowly as I could, like a safe-cracker, backing up if I thought I heard even the whisper of signal. It was a tedious exercise, and so far I'd never found anything apart from the signal broadcast by the Agency, which played nothing but a five-minute message about where and how to receive medical care, rations, and the life-saving serum. It looped endlessly. I could recite it by heart.

I closed my eyes, listening to the static hiss and woof in my ear.

A chorus of "Surprise!" rang out from the television. Arie cut it off by jabbing the fast-forward button.

"Another one," said Arie. "Did anyone care about anything besides birthdays back before?"

I felt it almost the instant he said it. Another thing that was taken from us, but something we didn't remember. We knew what birthdays were. We knew what typically happened at birthday parties, but nobody celebrated them anymore. Our records didn't show birthdays—only ages. The day we got our serum injections—that was everyone's collective birthday.

I saw the muscle in Arie's jaw tense, and I understood that he felt it, too. Longing, maybe anger, but mostly the strange sense of losing something you couldn't remember—a feeling that any day could be your birthday and you wouldn't even know it. Nothing distinguished one day from the next. There was nothing special, nothing to look forward to. And maybe that would be fine if you didn't know what you were missing, but we did. We knew such things in a general sense, the same way someone can know the rules of baseball without ever playing it. We saw the people in the home movies unwrapping presents and having cake, and that made us feel like no one wanted to throw us any parties, and no one ever would. We all carried it—a longing for things and people forgotten but nevertheless missed.

I decided then that I would throw Arie a birthday party. There wouldn't be cake or balloons of course, but I'd figure out some way to make it special.

Arie fast-forwarded through a few DVDs and then

plugged in a memory card.

"Ah, here we go," he said. I got up from the radio and went to Arie's side. The video showed a man lying in a hospital bed. He was damp and pallid. A young woman's voice narrated.

"Wave to the camera, David!"

David flipped the bird.

"He's not feeling too hot," said the woman. "We're going to get some fluids in him and the doctors are doing some tests and he should be home soon. Anyhoo, toodles!"

She turned the camera on herself to wave goodbye. Her eyes were brown and her hair was blond. She wore makeup. She smiled, but you could tell she didn't mean it. She was tired. The video ended.

"Time stamp is February 15th," Arie said grabbing his pencil and notebook.

"Day after Valentine's Day?"

"Psh," said Arie. "No. I mean this is the first wave."

"Oh, right."

He selected the next file. It showed the blond woman holding the camera on herself again, only now she wore a white paper hospital mask and no makeup. She pulled it down to her chin and sighed.

"I haven't been very good about recording," she said. "I can't believe what's going on."

She looked to have aged several years. Worry showed at the corners of her mouth. Dark circles under her eyes.

"David's in quarantine; they won't let me visit him." She turned away from the camera for a few seconds, then she was back. "School's canceled. They won't say for how long. I haven't been out of the house for three days." The woman stared down for several seconds at something off camera, and then shrugged.

The video ended.

"Now we're at March first," Arie said pointing at the list of files. "That takes us to—what? Two weeks out?"

Arie selected the next file.

The lady with the camera again. "Guys, I'm really scared. This is serious. Like serious-serious. People are dying and—"

She covered her eyes and sobbed. The camera wandered away from her face for a while. Then she pointed it at herself again.

"They think it's spread through the air. We don't even know if they know, so how can we—"

There was pounding on our front door and shouting outside.

"What's that?" Arie asked. He paused the video.

More pounding. It had to be a goon squad. No one would be pounding on the door like that at this hour.

"Turn off the television!" I shouted. "Turn everything off! And hide!"

Arie frantically shut down his electronics. I ran through the house shutting off the lights, first upstairs and then down, and then my pulse accelerated as I crept in the darkness toward the window at the front of the house.

A heavy curtain was drawn across the window. I parted it just enough to see the porch.

There was a young woman there. She had a gash on her head and her nose was bloody. Blood trailed down her face and neck.

"Help!" she shouted into surface of the door. "Please help me!" She glanced back over her shoulder then pounded with increased intensity. She knew we were inside. She'd seen our lights.

Arie reappeared. In the darkness, I could barely make

him out.

"Are you going to let her in?" he whispered.

"No," I said. "It's too dangerous.

"Well we can't just leave her out there," he said, gesturing at the door. "We've gotta do something."

"We have to protect ourselves, Arie. You know that. Whoever she's running from will end up in here."

"But, but we have to help her. Hide her or—"

"No, Arie, you go hide."

"But—"

"Go!"

As he left, I sat in front of the door, my back against it. The woman pounded on the door, and could feel the impact in my ribcage. I thought she might break down the door. A few moments later, I heard men's voices. The young woman screamed and ran off. There was shouting somewhere down the street, and then it was quiet again.

I shut my eyes. Arie was disappointed and hurt. I could tell. He always wanted to help everyone, but he didn't know how dangerous that could be. Sometimes it seemed risky to go and collect our rations or even just step out of the house. There was never enough food or fuel or clean water. I'd heard that we lived in one of the safer Zones, but still we saw fights in the streets in broad daylight, and when it was dark, the desperate and murderous preyed on the unsuspecting and the weak.

The Agency sent goons to patrol the Zones, but they weren't disciplined or even trained, and they were known to cause as much trouble as they prevented. If we got involved every time someone cried for help, it would soon be us pounding on some random door and disappearing in the middle of the night. I wanted to help people. Of course I did. And I was proud of Arie for wanting that, too, but we had to take care of ourselves first. That was the world we lived in. Why did the woman have to come to our house? Who was she, and what would become of her? I tried to drive her from my mind, but she wouldn't go easily.

In the morning, I woke up on the floor in front of the door. The electricity was off again, and Arie was asleep. I went quietly out onto the porch with a wet rag and wiped away the blood.

CHAPTER 4

Arie and I didn't talk much that morning. He had powdered eggs and tea for breakfast, then busied himself in the den, reading and filing the magazines he'd found. Arie had amassed hundreds of magazines and newspapers just in the previous nine months, to say nothing of the videos and computer documents and all the electronic devices he'd found. He kept diaries he'd found, too, and appointment books, photos, and letters. Anything about the year or so before the pandemic—he read it, collated it, curated it.

There were documents at the Agency depot that told the official history of the pandemic, but they were unsatisfying, suspiciously vague, and—as Arie had discovered—frequently inaccurate. So, Arie devoured any scrap of information he could find. He filled one bookshelf and then another. Now his magazines and materials nearly filled three floor-to-ceiling shelf units in the den, and still he searched the neighborhoods outside our Zone boundaries whenever he could.

I had tried several times to make him give up the searching, but he wouldn't. I tried to make him search less frequently, but at times it was all he ever wanted to do. And so, we fell into a kind of rhythm. I insisted on moving quickly, quietly, and being as careful and safe as we could. Arie agreed to that at least. Some days I almost felt safer out there in the empty neighborhoods. There were certainly fewer people to deal with, fewer riots and enforcement sweeps, but the stakes were undoubtedly higher—the lone patrol we saw and that pack of dogs would probably be enough to keep Arie home for at least a couple weeks. I was glad for that.

In the afternoon it was cloudy and cold, but the chores were done. We had water and supplies to last a few days, and so Arie continued working quietly and intently, indexing and cross-referencing his findings. It was as if he thought he could construct a printed, freestanding memory of everything that had happened before Year One.

In a way, we were searching for ourselves, too. There was always a chance that we'd walk into a house and see dust-caked portraits of our younger, happier selves. We had no idea where we'd come from originally—it was said that the Agency had corralled all survivors into a system of Zones; we could have come from anywhere. But the minuscule chance of happening upon the house that used to belong to us was one of the few things that kept me going along, despite my fear.

That evening, as I was making soup for supper, Arie came into the kitchen and sat in the bay window with his knees drawn up nearly to his chin. He opened the girl's flowered diary I found, holding it close to his face and straining in the failing gray light to read the former owner's squiggly cursive. I stayed quiet, waiting for him to speak first. I stirred the soup, and the room gradually filled with its aroma.

"The Sky Dreamer," Arie blurted.

He looked up from the diary. And I looked at him.

"The Ferris wheel we saw," he said. "That's what

they called it."

"Sky Dreamer," I repeated, nodding.

"She rode it," he said, holding up the diary. "She went with her friends."

"Anything interesting?" I asked. "Anything important?"

Arie shrugged. "Nah."

"Soup's ready," I said, turning the handle on the little propane burner we used to cook. It was just old canned tomato soup, but it steamed invitingly as I poured it into bowls. There were a few half-stale flour biscuits. Now that winter was approaching, we had to dress warmly, even indoors, with sweaters and scarves and fingerless gloves. The soup would warm us up.

"You should write down what happened with the dogs," Arie said.

I shrugged.

"You'll want to know how you got those scars," he said, gesturing at my bandaged leg. "You've got to write down the everyday things, too."

It was Arie's idea to keep journals. The Agency said we didn't need to. In fact, they gently discouraged it, said it would only confuse us when we woke up again each year. They said it was their job to keep our important information for us, stored on the microchips beneath our skin. Name, address, family, allergies, medical conditions. Every year, when we forgot, they gave it all back to us. But we lost everything else. Things we did, people we met, our experiences. We had one year of memories, and then we started over again. That is what they told us.

Arie said we had to write every day, that it was important. He said it would be a way to get to know ourselves again after waking up. He said it would put us ahead of the game, too, that it would help us survive in the harsh circumstances of life in the Zones. And that was true enough—there was so much to know, so many shortcuts and tricks to get by. But Arie thought it was more than that. He wouldn't say what it was, but I knew he had other reasons for keeping his journals.

I had a hard time with it, though. It took time, for one thing, a commodity that often ran short, and Agency couldn't resupply it. It was also hard to believe it would make any difference, and the Agency personnel were always announcing that they were close to fixing the memory problems of the serum.

"When was the last time you journaled, anyway?" asked Arie when I handed him a bowl of the soup.

It was so like him to check up on me that way. As though he were the one in charge. There was so much in his personality that was different from mine—he could be bossy, stubborn, and sometimes arrogant. Where did that come from?

"Don't worry," I said. "I will."

"Mom. Promise me."

"Okay, okay," I said taking a spoonful of soup. "I will."

"Okay, but really do it," he said. "It's everything. What's the point of doing anything if we're not going to remember it? Having a family? Living a life? How can we know who we are without memories? Really, how can you love someone you don't even remember?"

I blew on my soup. "It's worked all right for us."

Arie sighed and sipped his. "Yeah, but it's like we die every year. We're not the same people; we don't exist anymore, but we keep on living. Whoever we are just disappears, but we don't die. This started with a plague, a sickness, but it's the zombie apocalypse now. We're all just mindless zombies doing whatever the Agency tells us to."

"It's not gone," I said. I took his hand. "You said yourself. The memories are still there. We just have to unlock them. And we will. But until then, we still have each other, and that's what counts, whether I recognize you next year or not. Some things you know even when you don't remember. Some things can't be erased."

He nodded.

"Do you think we ever rode one?" he asked.

"Rode what?"

"A Ferris wheel. The Sky Dreamer."

I shrugged. "I probably did. But I'd never take you."

"What?" He lifted his head. "Why not?"

"You get woozy just turning in a circle," I said. "You'd probably barf all over me."

He laughed a little. I chucked him on the shoulder.

"I wonder if that ever happened," he said.

"I don't know. Maybe we'll remember next year."

There was a familiar knock at the door. Two quick taps, a pause, and then one more. It was Gary Gosford, the Agency man. He always knocked that way. I went to the door and opened it.

"Hello, Alison," he said, his thick eyebrows knitted. "I heard you got hurt."

Gary wore a long coat of gray wool and a dark felt Homburg. He had a round face that was friendly but with a touch of melancholy. Around his waist he carried the spread of middle age, and his shoulders were rounded.

I held up a hand, tried to wave off his concern.

"Why didn't you have them fetch me?" he complained. "You still have no idea what a difference it makes having a friend in the Agency. I'm sure I could've helped."

Unlike the other Agency enforcers we knew and had heard about, Gary treated those of us in the general population like real people—especially, it seemed, when it came to Arie and me. He occasionally brought us extra rations, and sometimes he'd help us with big chores and heavy lifting.

Gary and the others who worked for the Agency had been certified as being in remission and no longer needing the annual serum treatments. Because he could move freely among those who carried the virus, and because he'd been able to keep the memories he'd accumulated since being Remission Certified, Gary and others like him were culled from the general population to act as Agency supervisors, liaisons, and security personnel.

Gary was a senior supervisor in our Zone, some kind of middle administer and probably very busy, but he took time once in a while to check on Arie and me. Maybe he knew how difficult it must be for a single mom living in the Zones, and he really just wanted to help, but I often suspected Gary was interested in more than just friendship. It could never happen, of course—he was Remission Certified and I was in gen-pop, but I had to admit it was mildly flattering.

"We're fine, Gary. Really. You're busy. There was no reason to bother you."

Gary stepped onto the threshold. He didn't come all the way in, but he touched my shoulder. "You're really all right?"

"Completely. Just cuts and scratches."

"What happened?" he asked. "Dogs, I heard?"

Gary was, technically, the same as the thugs who rough-handled us at the infirmary and the rollers in the armored vehicle we crossed paths with the day before—

those we called goons. Gary was a goon. He dressed much better, but he did work for the Agency. Still, I trusted him. He knew about Arie's collection, which he could probably find a way to construe as against the rules, but he'd never said a word about it. Aside from Arie, he really was the best friend I had.

"This is unacceptable," said Gary, shaking his head. "I'm gonna order up a few extra teams this week. It's bad enough dealing with some of the people in gen-pop. Now we've got rabid dogs running around?"

"That's nice, Gary, but it was our fault. We were down by the river bottoms, looking for asparagus. Not a big deal."

"Oh, not a big deal? You could have been killed."

Arie sidled up next to me. "Hey, Mr. G."

"Hey, Arie. How's it going?"

"Pretty good."

Gary's eyes went to the bandages on Arie's hands and arm. "You, too? Your mom was just telling me you guys got into some dog trouble."

"She told you?" asked Arie, one eyebrow lifted.

"Yes, Arie, I told Mr. Gosford—"

"Gary."

"—that we were down in the river bottom looking for asparagus and we got jumped by those dogs. Good lesson learned, right? But we'll live, right?"

Arie's eyes narrowed for a nearly imperceptible, but then he nodded.

"Yeah, but you guys are lucky," said Gary. "Coulda been much worse. Next time you get an asparagus craving, let me know." He chuckled. "I'll come with you."

Arie nodded, then gestured at Gary's hand and the cloth sack he held. "Whadja bring us?"

"Arie!" I chastised.

Gary smiled. "As a matter of fact, I bought a few things." He held out the sack.

"Gary, you know you don't need to bring us anything."

"Eh. It's no trouble."

Arie snatched the bag from him and peeked inside. "Yes. Peanut butter!" He rummaged the sack as he went to the kitchen.

"I know you don't like peanut butter, Alison, but there's some other things in there. Some soap. It's lavender, I think. And some flour. Oh, and sugar—a cup or two at least. And some other stuff."

"You're spoiling us," I told him. "But thanks, Gary. For everything."

"I gotta go," he said.

I was almost glad—I couldn't wait to get my hands on that soap. It might be nice to smell good for a bit, but we'd probably end up trading away most of the items—there was no sense in having luxuries when we could trade them for necessities. Maybe I could just smell the soap, then trade it for eggs. But Arie was probably already halfway through that jar of peanut butter.

"I'm just glad you guys are okay. I gotta run. But I am gonna send a team or two to find these dogs. Or maybe I'll just have to go after them myself."

I grinned and Gary put on his hat. He turned to go but then stopped and faced me.

"Seriously," he said. "Next time you get into any kind of trouble, tell someone to go and find me. If I'm available, I'll be there as soon as I can."

"Okay. I will. Thanks."

Gary had visited the house the first day we moved in, not too long after we'd recovered from our treatment and completed orientation at the start of the new year.

It felt so long ago. Arie had been in the backyard working on an old bike he'd found half buried in dead bindweed vines. I was unpacking and sorting rations and supplies on the living room floor when Gary came in the front door. He didn't knock. He just walked in. At first I thought it was Arie and I screamed when I realized it was a stranger. I instinctively grabbed something to defend myself with—a small candlestick.

Gary hurriedly reached beneath the lapel of his long coat and fished out a clear plastic ID badge on a lanyard. It was inscribed with the Agency seal and a barcode with numbers.

"It's okay," said Gary, his voice raised but not threatening. "I'm with the Agency. My name's Gary. Gary Gosford. They told you that name, right?"

I clutched the candlestick like a tiny baseball bat.

"I'm with the Agency," he repeated quietly and more slowly. He removed his hat and held out the badge again. "I'm Gary. You're Alison. It's okay. I should have knocked first. I'm sorry."

Unlike most of the other people I'd encountered around the Zone that first week, Gary was well fed and dressed in clean clothing. I set the candlestick down, but within reach. Gary tucked the badge back into his coat. I watched him carefully.

"I really didn't mean to scare you," he said. "I'm just so used to walking in. I'll knock next time. I'm your senior supervisor."

"Well, I guess you know who I am," I said.

"Yes. Alison. I know. And your son is Arie. It's nice to see you again. You look well."

"They already told us about the rules," I said. "We've been careful. They gave us rations."

"Yes," he said. "That's good."

He worried the brim of the Homburg in his hands.

"Don't worry," said Gary. "You're not in trouble."

"Then what are you doing here?" I asked.

"Well, I know you don't remember me," he said, "but just a few weeks ago we were pretty good friends."

It was so disorienting. To hear someone say something like that—someone you don't recognize at all. Someone you don't know.

And I didn't believe him at the time. I doubted what he was saying, even though it had to be true.

He'd opened his mouth to speak, but then he stopped himself. He looked down and then up. He smoothed his hair. I waited.

"Awkward, isn't it?" he said. "I get it. This is all very new to you, I know, but as a senior supervisor in this Zone, it's my job to help, to make sure your needs are being met."

"Okay."

There was an uncomfortably long pause. Then finally Gary drew a long breath. "Well, can I visit you, then? I used to come by a couple times a week."

At the time, I didn't want him to, didn't want to invite some stranger into our lives, but it didn't seem like I had a choice, and I was very alone and confused.

"Sure," I told him without enthusiasm. "Whatever you say."

He seemed nice, harmless, maybe even a little lonely. But still, he was an Agency man, and that came with a lot of power. Already I'd heard whispers that you couldn't trust the Agency people. Already I'd heard people calling them goons. At first I only wanted to avoid breaking the rules or making Gary angry at me, but over time he really had become a friend to us, just like he'd said that day we moved in. I felt a lot of guilt about how I'd treated him those first few days.

I stood at the door as Gary went down the porch stairs.

"Tell Arie to go easy on that peanut butter," he said over his shoulder.

I waved goodbye and shut the door. Then I went to the kitchen, where Arie was gulping what I suspected was a cup of tea, syrupy with sugar. I laughed at him and sniffed deeply at the paper-wrapped soap.

"Where do you supposed he gets soap like this? Are there certain people who are getting nice soap and others who get none? Who was this for?"

"I don't know," said Arie, "but I'm gonna eat their peanut butter."

"Don't get too attached to the other stuff," I told him. "We're trading most of it."

"You know," Arie said, with a wink, "I bet we could get him to bring us a lot more stuff. He likes us. He likes you."

"We're fine," I said. "Whatever extra he brings us is great. But you're right. He does like us."

"Especially you," Arie teased.

I reached over and tousled his hair.

CHAPTER 5

A few days passed, and our injuries began to feel a little less raw.

"I'm going out to pick up our rations," I told Arie as I pulled on my coat and wrapped a scarf around my neck. I thought I'd try riding my bike again.

He didn't answer.

"Arie? You in here?"

I found him in the den, crouching by the window that overlooked the backyard.

He turned to me and put a finger to his mouth.

"Shh," he whispered.

"What is it?" I asked, walking closer. "Is something wrong?"

"Get down," he said, motioning.

I crouched and Arie motioned me to the window.

"Look," he said.

He carefully pushed the curtain slightly aside.

"What? I don't see anything," I said.

"The apple," Arie said.

I hadn't seen it at first, but at the edge of the back porch there sat a red apple.

"What's that doing there?"

"Just watch," whispered Arie, stifling a laugh.

I watched the apple. Nothing happened.

"Arie—"

"Just wait," he said.

We sat there for maybe a minute. Then, a hint of movement in the back corner of the backyard caught my eye, and a girl of about seven or eight years old poked her head out from around the old sugar maple tree there. She poked her head out, then retreated. She did this a few times, then stepped out from behind the tree. Her face and hands were filthy, and her hair was curly and blond, like buttered noodles, and when she stepped into the sun, it lit up like an angel's halo. She stood still and looked around—checking, watching. Then she crept like a cat to the porch, snatched the apple, and ran away through an open space in the back fence.

Arie stood up, smiling. "I've been leaving food for her for a couple weeks now. She always comes around about this time."

"She just came over and asked for food?" I asked.

"No, no," said Arie. "She thinks she's being really sneaky. One day a while ago I was working on my bike out there and I came inside to grab a wrench—left my lunch on the porch. It was a biscuit with some butter and cheese on it. When I came back, it was gone. Happened a couple other times. I'd turn my back and my lunch would disappear. She really is a little ninja, but one day I finally spotted her. But I turned away fast, pretended not to notice. So now I've been leaving something on the porch every couple days. As soon as I come inside, she sneaks up and swipes it."

"I've never seen her. Who is she?"

"Not sure, but she keeps coming back. Sly little thing. I've been thinking about talking to her, finding out where she lives or whatever."

"Arie, I don't know about this. What if it makes

trouble for us?"

"Trouble? She's a little kid. What trouble?"

"I don't know. What if she breaks in?"

"Well, quite frankly, she coulda done that already. But she's just hungry, obviously." He grinned. "Maybe she can become my new little sister."

"I wish you wouldn't encourage her. You should be eating that food yourself. We barely have enough as it is."

"It makes me happy," said Arie, "and that's as good as food, sometimes."

Even in the few months we'd been together, Arie already knew how to manipulate me. It was hard enough finding moments of happiness, and Arie he knew I wouldn't deny him. You just never knew who you could trust, though—even when it came to little kids. We'd seen so many bad things. The world was such a very dangerous place. The best way to a safe, was to stay low. Stay out of the way. Look out for yourself.

I sighed. "Just be careful," I said.

"I always am."

*

The line had maybe a hundred people in it when I arrived. I stood behind a tall man with a bushy beard and wild auburn hair. On his shoulders was perched a small girl who had the same wild hair. She looked to be four or five years old.

"What's the hold-up?" I asked him.

"Who knows." He peered up at the little girl. "Tell 'em to hurry up, will ya, Penny?"

Penny leaned over shouted, "G-o-o-o!"

I scrunched my nose at her. "Your daughter?"

"S'what they tell me." He grinned.

A joke everybody had heard before, but I nodded

and smiled back. "I have a son. But he's older. I can't imagine what it's like for the little ones."

"Oh, no," he said, "this is the way to go."

He swayed a little but held onto Penny's ankles. She giggled and held his head tighter.

"I figured she'd be real messed up," he said, "but, you know, they're not going to remember anything. They start fresh. Isn't that right, Pen?"

She drummed unmercifully on his head. He was unfazed.

"I can make all the typical parenting mistakes but it won't matter for you because you won't remember, will ya?"

She drummed harder, pulled his hair.

The line moved a little. We took a few steps forward and craned our necks to see ahead.

"Finally," said the man.

"Finally," Penny mimicked.

The Agency Depot was the only place to get food and supplies in quantities sufficient to feed more than a single person. The Agency scanned our electronic chips, and these were used to withdraw rations of various kinds on a monthly schedule. They furnished the basics—rudimentary medical supplies, sanitary goods, and fuel for our stoves and heaters.

They gave us food, too, although it consisted mostly of staples and was very plain. There were rations of flour, cornmeal, rice, and beans. There were dehydrated meals with pasta and potatoes, and soy powder to make a sort of chalky milk drink for protein. In the growing season there might be heads of pithy cabbage, white onions, or grotesquely overgrown winter squash.

"So, she didn't have a hard time?" I asked the man. "At the beginning of the year?"

"Nah. Like I said, the kids take to it better than we do. They don't question. They believe everything. 'Hey kid, I'm your dad.' 'Okay, get me a drink of water. Wipe my bum. Tuck me in.' It doesn't slow them down."

"Right."

"They'll be the first generation to grow up without the mistakes of their parents," he said. "Of course, I can't remember my parents, either, but I figure the psychological damage was already done when the virus hit."

The way he looked at her and talked to her—even the way he gripped her ankles—I could tell he was smitten. Nine months ago, like all of us, he'd woken up and not known Penny at all, and now she was daddy's little girl, at least for a few more months. I knew just how he felt.

It wasn't like that for everyone, though. For some, the fog of forgetting was too deep, the threads of attachment too strained. Or maybe mistakes were made—kids placed with people who weren't really their parents. We'd never know. The Agency ran a home for orphans and the kids whose parents could not perform their duties, but I suspected lots of those parents simply would not. I thought that was maybe better than being in homes where they weren't cared for. I didn't know. Rumor had it the Agency would try to place the children in the home with their parents every year. Did it click some years and not others? The Agency seldom answered questions like that and never volunteered any information.

The line lurched forward, but then there was shouting ahead. Two Agency goons had taken hold of a young man and were fighting him into the building. He shouted in protest. Those in line strained to see, standing on their toes and leaning.

"What's going on?"

"I can't hear what they're saying," said the man. "Maybe he's got a ripped chip."

I glanced up at Penny and the man turned her away from the commotion. Two more Agency guards showed up and the young man was overwhelmed. They got out their clubs and then I looked away, too, but I glanced back when his shouting stopped. The man was limp and I watched them drag him away. Nobody said anything and neither did I.

The line moved again and the man and his daughter were waved past the barricades. An Agency worker approached with a scanning wand. The man tilted his head. It was a peculiar motion, the head tilt. It was diffident, a little like bowing for prayer, and I'd often thought it would perhaps strike someone else as odd, but to us it was perfectly natural and we did it without thinking. Bow, scan, move along.

The same worker waved me through and I was scanned and then I moved along, too. When I bowed my head, I saw spots of blood on the pavement from where the young man had been subdued.

I collected my provisions without reading the labels and tucked them beneath my coat. I made it back through the barricades, and as I rushed to my bicycle, I saw the man with the girl on his shoulders. I waved to them. The man lifted his chin and showed me a sad smile. Penny waved. She looked happy.

When I was alone, well away from the Depot, I pulled over and checked the provisions. It was rice and black-eyed peas. Two pounds of each. Not much, but I could pad out the rice with what we had at home and probably make it until the next distribution. I put them

45

in my backpack with the books I'd brought from home. Then I kept riding.

There was never enough of anything. We almost never had enough cooking oil or salt. Most people went months without fruit—even the canned kind. Liquor was so rare it was as though it simply no longer existed, like cable television and the Internet and birthdays.

So, we traded. We learned who might have extra and who never did. And we learned who traded supplies for skills, too. There was an older man in town who mended clothing and shoes. A lady down the street from us had located a small flock of chickens holed up somewhere just across the Zone boundaries. Each morning she sent her children to gather the eggs—I heard it was over a mile each way. And I'd heard about a person in my neighborhood who collected wild honey, but I never found out who it was.

I rode out past the burned-out factories on the edge of town and got on the highway. It was choked with a permanent traffic jam of cars and busses. They'd sat motionless for so long the sun had dulled their paint. The weeds growing up through the cracks in the pavement were so tall and thick I had to weave my way between them, too. After a few miles, I got off the highway and rode to a desolate drive-in movie theater where there was an enormous white and gold RV, parked as if ready to watch that evening's feature.

Inside, Donna lived surrounded by her cats and her books.

Most of the cats scattered or dove beneath the RV as I rode up. A few sat in the dust and watched me. One ran up and rubbed itself against my ankle and walked a figure-eight through my legs. I reached up to knock on the door but before I could, Donna opened it—just a crack wide enough for her to see me.

"Hi, Donna. It's Alison."

She stood there peering through the space of the partially open door, blinking at me through one thick lens of her wire-framed spectacles. I saw that in one hand she held a hardback book with a finger inserted to hold her place.

"What are you reading today?" I asked.

She blinked at me like an owl.

"I have a few books for you," I said. "And some beans."

"Let me see," she said, opening the door a little more.

"The books? Or the beans?"

"The books."

I unshouldered my pack and rummaged inside.

"I found these," I said, offering her the books. One was a collection of Isaac Asimov stories and the other two were spy novels.

She inspected the first spy novel and handed it back with a slight shake of her head. The second one, too. When she saw the Asimov collection, her expression changed slightly. The hint of a smile.

"Notebooks?" she asked.

"Yes, please."

She went inside. The door swung closed but not all the way. I peeked into the RV. I'd never been in. The only light inside seeped in through the few windows and was filtered through heavy curtains. From what I could see, there was little in there apart from a couch completely walled around with piles of books. Books on shelves and others in boxes and there were tall but orderly stacks, too. She must have moved like a phantom in there to avoid knocking them over.

Donna came back with three spiral notebooks. I was

going to give them to Arie for his birthday. With all the journaling and note-keeping he did, he'd need them. She held them out and I gave her the paperback books.

"Thanks, Donna."

"Mm."

"Here," I said. "This, too." I held up the sack of black-eyed peas.

"I don't need those."

"Sure you do. When's the last time you went to the depot? Would you rather some rice? You have to eat."

Without taking it from my hand, she turned the packet of beans so that she could squint at the label. She made the little head shake again.

"Just take them," I said, but she was already shutting the door.

*

On my trip back, a few miles from my house, I saw a bulky figure waddling between the tall, winter-dry weed stalks that grew up through the pavement.

It was Ruby.

I considered passing her by, but before I could decide for sure, I was steering the bike in her direction and I knew she'd spotted me. She limped along. When I got close enough, she showed me her grin and nodded, but there was something cursory in her greeting, something dismissive. Her face was florid and wet with sweat.

I swung the bike around and came up alongside her at a distance, pedaling slowly. She was breathing hard.

"Hey," she yelled. "You. Get over here."

"What are you doing out here?" I asked.

"That's nonaya business," she said. "But I need that favor."

"Why?" I coasted closer to her. "What's going on?"

We came to an intersection and Ruby slowed so that she could glance over her shoulder. I looked in that direction but saw nothing.

"Someone after you?"

"I gave 'em the slip back at the depot, but they'll be along soon enough."

"Goons."

She nodded with her sly grin.

"What do they want?"

"I think they found out I carry this piece," she said, patting her hip. "Been after me a couple days. I need you to take it."

"What? Your gun? No. Just get rid of it."

She clicked her tongue. "Not a chance."

"What'll they do if they catch you with it?"

"Well," she said, "they ain't gonna take me dancing."

"Then ditch it," I said. "Hide it somewhere for a while."

She pressed her lips together and shook her head. "Can't risk it. It'll get found or I'll forget where I stuck it. And it'll get rusted. You don't know what it took to get it, and now I'm not going to lose it. You're going to take it for me, and I'm gonna get it back from you."

We looked down the street again. Four or five blocks back, I thought I saw something moving among the hulks of the derelict cars.

"That's them," said Ruby.

She squatted between the weed stalks. I got off my bike and laid it down. Then I crouched in the road with her.

"They haven't seen you, don't know ya. You got to get going now," she said. She wetted her lips and dug around under the flap of her coat and produced the pistol.

It was worn and pitted with age. The handle grips were held on with friction tape. She held it in both hands, turned it over.

"Here then," she said, holding it out. "Take it."

"No way!"

"Listen, Missy," she said, poking her stumpy finger at my face. "I saved your life. You owe me one. You take this gun and go on home."

"What if they stop me?"

"They don't know you, and it ain't you they're looking for. Now take it."

She passed it to me and I took it. It was heavier than I thought it would be. She fumbled under her coat again and came out with a small bundle of greasy cloth.

"Bullets. Take 'em."

They clattered like marbles in the cloth.

"If you double-cross me," said Ruby holding up the stumpy index finger, "you'll be sorry."

I started to answer, but couldn't.

"Where do you live?"

I hesitated. The last thing I wanted was this woman knowing where I lived.

"Damn it, where d'ya live?"

I told her.

"I know that street. Go straight home," she ordered. Then she knitted her brows as though she might reconsider. "Get going. If I'm not there before dark, just hide it. I'll deal with these knuckleheads. Don't let 'em see you."

I walked my bike away from the intersection, staying low and watching down the street. When I thought I'd gone far enough, I got on the bike and rode.

The street was lined with volunteer elm trees growing up twisted and unpruned. On the tips of the leaves the blush of autumn was spreading. Between the trees there sprouted small jungles of unkempt ornamental shrubs and weeds gone to seed. Soon the warm colors of fall would displace the last of the greenery, and then the leaves would be gone. It wouldn't be much longer after that and our memories would be gone, too.

Out on the street there was a man in a filthy and ragged ski parka skulking through the deepening shadows. Probably just another wanderer or maybe even someone like me on the way home, but you could never be too safe. Ordinarily, if I were alone, I'd dive for cover and stay quiet at the sight of somebody like that, but I thought of the cool metal weapon pressed against my tummy at the top of my jeans, and I wondered if it could protect me. I put my hand on the grip and watched the man pass by. He didn't seem to notice me. It occurred to me that I wasn't even exactly sure how to shoot the gun, and if I tried to pull it out, it might go off in my pants. And I knew I could be hauled off by the goons for merely having it on my person. Hauled off and never seen again, and Arie might never even be told what happened. I felt like I could barely breathe.

I'd been home for over an hour, pacing, before Ruby showed up. I saw her from the window and went out to meet her. Her right eyelid looked like plum.

"Jesus, Ruby," I said. "What'd they do?"

"Let's have that piece," she said.

"Yes, please take it." I reached under my shirt.

"Not out here, you dummy. Go inside."

I stood there for a second.

"You want the whole neighborhood to know?" she asked. "People watch. They see. They talk."

We stepped inside and Ruby shut the door.

I pulled on the handle and Ruby grabbed the gun away almost before the barrel cleared the waist of my pants. In another second she'd hidden it under the great flaps of her coat.

"What happened?" I asked.

"Oh," she scoffed, "they shook me down. You know how they are. Puny men with badges. They were plenty disappointed I didn't have nothing on me. Said I musta hid it somewhere. So, they give me this shiner."

She fished her eyeglasses from a pocket and wiped the hazy lenses with the tail of her shirt, which didn't clear them up at all. Then she nodded to me.

"How'd they find out about your gun?"

"Oh, probably someone narc'ed on me. I got enemies. And them goons don't like me much to begin with, neither."

"I saw them use a stun gun on a guy across the street a couple months ago," I told her.

Ruby scoffed. "They do a lot worse than that."

"Like what?" I said.

She grinned, shook her head. "You don't wanna know, but I'm sure you can guess."

That was true.

"Watcha got to drink?"

She didn't wait for me to answer, just waddled through the house headed toward the kitchen, not seeming to care whether I was coming.

"Nice place," said Ruby.

I scurried behind her, wondering what Arie would think of this stranger flooding into the house.

"Wait," I said.

"What? I need a drink," she said.

"What can I get you? Something for your eye?"

"What, for this?" she said, pointing to her eye. "Nah,

he hit like a fifth-grader. I've had worse."

I believed it. "How about some water?" I asked.

She found the kitchen. "Yeah, all right. Unless you got something stronger."

"Stronger? No. Where would I get something like that?"

"Oh, it looks like you do just fine," she said, eyeing the shelves and cupboards.

For a woman with a limp, she was remarkably quick, moving through the kitchen and pulling out the drawers as though conducting an inspection. She opened a cupboard, pulled a packet of crackers part way out, then shoved it back. I couldn't decide if she was being rude or if it was her way of saying we were friends now, so I kept quiet.

"Yeah," she said. "Just fine."

"The cups are there by the sink," I said.

Ruby grabbed a cup and I dispensed some water from our plastic water can. She continued her inspection.

"Interesting," she said, pointing at the police scanners stacked on the fridge. She inclined her head to peep up at them through her bifocals.

"Yeah. Don't know why those are there."

"Uh huh," she said, moving on.

She found the shelf where I kept some of the things I'd collected from the abandoned houses—a silver-plated jewelry caddy in the shape of a cat, a pair of dentures, a paper fan—tchotchkes that had caught my eye. They weren't particularly useful or worth anything in trade, but I held my breath for a few seconds, hoping she wouldn't ask about them. She bent down and lifted her eyeglasses to see them closer.

"Pretty," she said, lifting the flowered tea cup I'd found the day the dogs attacked us.

"Are you finished?" I asked, reaching for her cup.

"No, not quite yet." She sipped at the water and turned away to keep me from taking it from her.

Arie had left a stack of magazines on the counter. Ruby fanned them out to see their covers, then plucked one from the pile. She held it at arm's length, tilted her head to read it.

Thankfully, Arie wasn't home. I was displeased with the way she so boldly rifled our things, but Arie would surely have lost his temper.

She shuffled around the table and headed for the den, with its quagmire of cables, adapters, and monitors. The shelves of books. The radio. I rushed around her to block the entrance.

"Whatcha got back there?" she asked, smiling.

"Nothing," I told her. "There's nothing back there."

Ruby knew the rules. Everybody did. It was the first thing they told you. Before you knew your name, before you knew what had happened, they told you the rules. Before we took our first steps into the murky dawn of our new and dismal lives, we'd already been told the rules three times. Obey Agency personnel. Be in by curfew. No stealing, no looting, no weapons. There were lots of rules in a book they'd given us, but they could also arrest you simply on suspicion of breaking the rules, or even suspicion of intending to break the rules. They could arrest you because they didn't like your face.

There was no way to prove that Arie's collection of documents and gadgets was illegal, or that we'd looted much of it from homes outside Zone boundaries. Gosford had seen the stash, watched it grow. He told me that some other Agency supervisor might find it all rather suspect, but I knew he wanted me to like him, and so he said nothing about it.

And now Ruby stood on tiptoe, looking over my shoulder into the den.

"Really, what is all that? Them computers and what not."

"I told you. It's nothing. Just things."

Ruby chuckled and handed me her cup. "Guess I'll be going, then, show myself out."

I stayed at the doorway to the den, watching as she walked back through the kitchen and into the living room, where she stopped abruptly and lowered her head.

I could see only her profile, and I stared at her, waiting for her to go out the door, wishing for her to leave, but then I noticed that her lips were moving. Like she was whispering to herself or praying. But no—she was reading.

When I followed her gaze, I saw it: my own journal, sitting out and open on the side table.

I scurried over, banging my hip on the counter and nearly tripping. Ruby heard me coming and leaned closer to the pages. I snatched up the journal and held it to my chest.

"What are you doing?" I demanded.

"That's yours, isn't it?"

"Yes, it's mine. And it's private."

Ruby lumbered over to our sofa and plopped into it.

"You know what, Alison," she said, rubbing her knee, "I'm angry. You think it's bad losing thirty or so years? Imagine losing twice that. A lifetime. And not only that. We lost the one advantage us old people had—our wisdom. I can't sleep through the night without getting up to pee three or four times. I'm slow as hell. And now, on toppa alla that, thanks to that serum, I'm dumber'n a teenager. Don't get old, Alison. It's the pits."

"It's bad for everyone. We're all at the same place,"

I said.

"What if I told you we aren't?" she sat up straight and spoke a bit quieter.

I crossed the room to be closer.

"The Agency knows a lot more'n they're telling us," Ruby said. "Shit, everyone knows, right? You know, don'tcha? Or at least suspect? I think everyone does. I think everyone suspects, but they're too busy tryna live and too scared to say anything."

"What do you mean?" I wanted her gone, but there was something about her, something that was subversive and hopeful at the same time.

"That journal's a good idea, you know." She jabbed her chin at my notebook. "Written in your own handwriting. You write everything down?"

"Try to."

She nodded slyly. "I oughta have my people doin' that."

"Your people?"

She chewed the inside of her cheek, thinking. "Listen. I got a place, Alison," she said, scooting forward on the couch. "I got a place on the outside. I've gathered up a few 'things,' too, and I'm making some plans. Folks like you and me—we don't like this bein' kept in the dark. I know you feel it. That's why you got them radios and whatnot. We're tired a'being sheeple, and we're hungry for light. You're smart. I could use your help. And I could help you, too. With lots of things. Food. Supplies. Get ya something decent to drink, for one. And more, maybe."

"What kind of plans?"

"I'll just say they're the kind 'a plans worth keeping secret, but ones I plan on remembering."

"Is it illegal?"

"It's hard to start a revolution when ya still salute the king." Ruby laughed.

"Is it safe?"

Ruby sighed. "No. It ain't. There's risks. But doing nothing is a risk, too. Wouldn't you agree?"

"No." I shook my head. "I'm not on my own. I have a son—he depends on me. I can't put him at risk. Don't tell me anything else." I stepped back. "I don't want to know."

Ruby looked at me for a while, shrugged, and said, "Suit yourself." Then she rocked a few times to raise up from the couch. "But if you ever change your mind, come out to the Harbor."

"Harbor?"

"That amusement park out by where we met them dogs that day. You know. Out where that rolly coaster and Ferris wheel is at. I'm there most days. Come on out if you change your mind."

I nodded—once. Then I went to the front door and opened it. Ruby stepped out onto the porch and then turned.

"One more thing," she said. "Don't be putting none of this in your diary. Don't put me in there. For my sake."

I nodded, and she started down the street. I was still watching her from the window when Arie rode up on his bicycle.

He paused and watched her go on down the block. Then he came up the stairs and opened the door.

"Hey," he said pointing his thumb over his shoulder, "wasn't that what's-her-name?"

"No," I answered.

"Then who—"

"It was no one."

CHAPTER 6

Two weeks later, all I wanted to do was go back. Rewind. The word repeated in my mind like a plea or a prayer. Rewind, rewind. To change the outcome, maybe, but mostly to be in those last moments again—days that had seemed so dreary and ordinary, but moments which now had become sacred. How I longed to live them over again. It wasn't possible, I knew, but that didn't stop me from wanting it. Rewind, rewind. It's all I thought about.

It started one morning as I passed Arie on the staircase. I was coming downstairs and he was heading up, his arms so full with stacked-up notebooks and magazines he had to hold them in place with his chin.

"What's all this?" I smiled, stopping a few stairs above him.

"New indexing system. I'm re-doing everything."

"Sounds like a big job," I said.

"Huge. You're going to love it." He continued past me and up the stairs. "And don't worry about lunch. I'll grab a bite later."

I didn't see him at all that day. I fetched water and firewood without him. I ate lunch alone. I worked around the house. When it was time for supper, I called up the stairs for him.

"I'm busy," he yelled down. "Can't stop now."

A couple hours later, Arie's door was shut when I took him a bowl of the soup I'd made. I knocked. No answer.

"Arie? Got some soup for you."

I knocked again. Nothing. I opened the door.

Arie sat cross-legged on the floor, three or four books open on his lap. A chaotic fortress of books and maps and photo albums stood around him. There was almost no place to walk or stand. Atop the stacks were candles whose lights leaned and flickered as I swung the door open. Shadows loomed and capered on the walls.

Arie was hunched forward, head down. His long bangs veiled his eyes. A pen was tucked behind one ear. He scanned the pages, jotting notes in a notebook every few moments.

"Arie."

He flipped a page but didn't look up.

"Arie," I repeated, louder.

He finally heard me and glanced up. "Oh. Hi. What's the matter?"

His face was pale and drawn, eyes glassy.

"I brought you something." I offered him the bowl. "You need to eat."

"Thanks." His eyes dropped back to the notebook. "Just put it over there. I've got some crackers and the last of the peanut butter."

I squeezed past the journals and files and set the bowl on the dresser. Cracker crumbs were spread across the blanket, and the little jar of peanut butter was half empty.

"Look at you," I said, taking a seat on a small empty spot on the bed. "You need a break. You can't keep working like this."

"Yeah," he said. "I'm almost finished for the day." His words sounded slurred.

I sat with him a few more minutes, trying to put my finger on what might be wrong with him, but I couldn't, and he didn't seem to notice me. He opened the books and magazines, jotting notes in the notebook. Finally, I got up and went to the door.

"Well, night, son," I said.

He murmured at me without looking up.

That night I awoke sweating and panting from some terrible dream, but unable to recall what had scared me so. The floorboards moaned and squawked as I left my bed to get some water. In the hallway, I saw a line of yellow light beneath Arie's door.

Thinking he might have fallen asleep and left some candles burning, I went to his door and listened for a moment. I heard the faint crackle of turning pages. I opened the door.

Arie was awake and in the same place as before, huddled over the papers and books. The bowl of soup remained on the dresser, undisturbed and cold. A few of the candles were still lit, burned down to cool flames in warm pools of wax that spread and dripped.

"Arie," I cried.

He raised his head. Deep dark bags drooped beneath his bloodshot eyes. He seemed barely able to hold himself up. The notebook was open to a page of dense, orderly writing, but I couldn't make it out in the dim candlelight.

"Yeah, yeah," he said. "I'll eat in a minute." Lowering his eyes to the notebook again, he said, "Just put it over there. I'm close. I've almost got it down."

"What are you doing? Do you know what time it is?"

"I'm seeing connections I never saw before," he said. "This is amazing."

"Go to bed right now," I said.

"In a second," he said.

"No. Now." I grabbed his arm and pulled him up.

Piles of books toppled and slid as he reluctantly allowed me to steer him to his bed. I cleared away the books and papers, and he lay down stiffly, muttering about his notes, about his indexing. I blew out the candles.

"Get some sleep," I told him. "You can finish later."

I went downstairs and got a drink of water. When I came back up, I heard the floorboards in his room creaking, and a moment later I saw candlelight flickering from the space beneath the door.

I sighed and went to bed.

In the morning I went to his room expecting to find him asleep on the floor amongst his papers. But he was still awake, staring transfixed at a magazine open on his lap.

"Did you sleep at all?" I demanded.

"You know what?" he said, tapping the open page of the magazine.

I looked closer. It was a photo of a line of people waiting to get into a hospital or shelter. There were soldiers with guns.

"You know what?" he said again. "I think I remember this. From before. This place, this day."

His face was paler now, and a thin layer of oily perspiration covered his skin.

"You're frying your brain is what you're doing. Leave it alone for a bit. I want you to go out to the Tanner's and help them fix that wheel barrow of theirs."

"Could you do it? I don't want to lose my place." His face was pallid. "I have a system going on." He waved his hands over the notebook as if casting a magic spell. "It's complicated. I need to finish."

"I can't go, Arie. I've got to soak a batch of beans, do the laundry, and caulk those windows downstairs before it gets seriously cold. And the bearings on that barrow need to be repacked. You're the only one who knows how—"

A drop of blood fell from his nose and splattered on the open magazine.

"Arie? You're bleeding. My god, you've got to stop. Now!"

He tilted his head back. "Oh, it's just a doze bleed," he said, pinching his nose. "Dis stuff is so dusty."

"You have to stop."

"I'll be done by dinner, okay? I promise."

I sighed. Where did his stubbornness come from?

"You'll be done by dinner," I repeated.

The afternoon was long and dim. The sky was gray the entire day. It was cold, and we'd probably see the first snows in another couple weeks. I got the water and soaked the beans and strung the laundry on lines we'd nailed up throughout the house. Then I went to the Tanners with Arie's tools. Together with Peggy and one of her boys we figured out how to pack the bearings and put the wheelbarrow back together, but our hands were raw and numb by the time we finished. At sundown I was tired and eager to eat.

I called Arie's name as I climbed the stairs. He didn't answer.

"You said you'd be done for dinner," I said, testily pushing open his door.

He was spread out on the floor on a layer of notebooks and papers, and he was convulsing. Paper crinkled and ripped beneath his kicking legs, and blood oozed from his ears and nose. A red foam bubbled out his mouth.

I screamed his name.

After crashing through the piles of books and paper, all I could do was cradle his bloody head in my lap. I didn't know what else to do. His body jerked and twisted. I brushed away the foam from his lips.

"Wake up, Arie," I cried. I said it again and again.

CHAPTER 7

When it was clear Arie wouldn't respond, I ran to a neighbor's house and pounded on their door. Arie's blood was on my hands, and I left smudges of it on the door. I thought of the woman who came to our house in the dark that night a week before. She was covered in blood, too, and she shouted desperately for help. Would my neighbors ignore me?

The door opened.

"Ron, thank god," I cried.

"Alison? What's going on?"

"It's Arie. He's—something's wrong with him. It's bad. You have to come."

"Let me get Steve. He's out back. We'll be right over."

When I returned to Arie's bedroom, his teeth had clamped down on his tongue, and his mouth was full of blood. His open eyes were glazed.

Ron and Steve appeared in the doorway of Arie's bedroom.

"He's having a seizure," Ron said.

Holding his head in my hands, I rocked back and forth, tears were dripping from my chin onto Arie's face. I could barely breathe.

"What do I do?" I begged.

They surveyed the room with incredulous looks, then turned to one another for explanation. Finding none, they turned to me.

"What happened?" asked Steve.

"I don't know. I don't know." I shook my head.

"We should take him to the infirmary," said Steve. "Right away."

Ron recoiled, and a look of dread flashed in his face for just a second. I understood. It was our instinct to avoid the sick, to fear any sign of illness. But Ron pressed his lips together, and he and Steve stepped into the room.

I got out of their way, and the two men struggled to hold onto Arie's kicking legs and flailing arms.

Time went fast and slow.

I held his head as they lifted him, but there wasn't room for all of us to move, so I let go. Arie's head lolled and he thrashed like a giant fish. It was only with great difficulty that they got him out of the house and down the street.

It was dark when we got to the infirmary, and Ron and Steve were soaked in sweat. Workers in hazmat suits swarmed out into the courtyard and surrounded us. Their headlamps cast wild distorted shadows onto the pavement and the cinderblock walls. Someone cut Arie's shirt off.

"I need to speak to Gary Gosford," I cried hoarsely. "Gosford. He's a—supervisor. Senior supervisor."

They ignored me, shouting for a stretcher, examining Arie, scanning his ID chip. Ron and Steve disappeared in the commotion. I would have, too. When the Agency workers turned their attention to me, they scanned me and fired off a series of questions about Arie. I may have answered some of them. I don't remember.

They placed Arie on a gurney and rolled him inside.

I tried to follow, told them to contact Gary, but they kept me out and the door shut behind them and locked. I stood there breathless, watching through the small window on the door. No one said anything to me. No one had told me I should wait or what would happen next.

They took my Arie away.

I stood there for a long while—staring at the empty hallway through the window of the door. After what could have been more than an hour, I realized that I was terribly cold. Physically, yes—I had no coat or even a jacket. But there was a cold, mental sluggishness deep inside me, too, which made it difficult to think or even move. I knew I'd be cold until I saw Arie again.

Rewind.

Day after day, I went back to the infirmary and waited outside with my dread and my regrets. I wished that I'd had one more look at him. Just to really see him. The small details—the flecks of color in the irises of his eyes, the dimple in his cheek. I wished that I'd held on a little longer when we'd last embraced, and that I wasn't always in such a rush to do other things. Maybe if I'd have been more firm in sending him to bed that night, or if I'd paid closer attention, I might have known he was so sick. If only I could go back—rewind, rewind.

After ten days with no information at all, my instincts told me to pound on the infirmary emergency admittance door until either they answered or it fell down. But I did not.

Instead I sat outside, staring at the stupid door. I stared at it so long that I memorized every detail of it. I stared at the edge where the paint was flaking off, at the residue of masking tape where a sign had once been posted. I stared at that infernal door so long that I saw it when I closed my eyes, when all I wanted to see was Arie's face.

I didn't know where my son was, and the only thing that stopped me from tearing the door down was knowing that they would keep him from me if I did.

So, I waited. Every day, outside, where the wind grew colder and colder. It tore at me, made my jaw and ears ache. I stayed all day and left only long after it was dark. I hardly ate. As soon as I could, I'd return to continue my vigil at the door.

The door would open once, maybe twice a day. Patients came and went, eyeing me warily. Workers and Agency goons appeared sometimes and I would rush to the door and question them. Sometimes I followed them as they walked away.

"My son. Arie. He was sick. He's in there. I just need to know if he's okay. I just want to see him."

I was never told anything.

"My Zone supervisor is Gary Gosford. Just tell him my name. Please. He said he'd help."

Nothing. The door was shut in my face.

Sometimes I was too numb to think. Not knowing was the worst. At the beginning of that year, I didn't know Arie. I'd been told he was my son. How strange it was to think about in that ghastly courtyard with the late autumn's chill settled around me like concrete. How strange it'd been to ask, "I have a son?" and then in the very next moment state, "I have a son."

I'd started to believe maybe there is something inside us that allows us to know when we love somebody. Something that we don't have to remember, something that is simply a part of us. The way I sometimes found things in the empty houses we searched, things that spoke to me. I couldn't explain it. But I would gladly give up my life for Arie. The boy I couldn't remember; the boy I could never forget. I loved him and I knew that I had before, even if I had to be reminded of it.

The other people in town watched me. From a distance. They were curious, maybe a little afraid. No one said anything to me.

On the fifteenth day, the sky was gray. A fog settled around the infirmary, so that I could not see the edges or top of the building, so that nothing existed but the cinder block wall and the hated door and me and the space between. I hunched in my coat with the collar turned up and an old scarf wrapped around my face. I sighed deeply, and from the scarf there came a cloud of whiteness like dragon smoke that dissolved in the air.

Everything was frozen. The ground, the water in the rain barrel at our house, the puddles along the streets, even the air. And me.

I gazed up into the fog and spotted a single snowflake falling. It was the only one I saw. It floated to the ground and landed at my feet. I watched for more, but none fell. At some point, maybe soon, the ground would be piled high with snow. But at that moment, only one snowflake had fallen.

The door opened. It was Gary Gosford.

I was on my feet in an instant. "Where's Arie?" I asked, rushing to the door.

Gary held the door open for me. "This way," he said.

He led me deep into the building to a small room that had a table and two chairs.

"I've been waiting for days," I said as I sat down. "For two weeks. Why won't anyone tell me what's going on?"

Gosford sat down across from me. His face was bristly with stubble.

"Alison, I'm so sorry. I didn't know. Things don't always work smoothly in the Agency. They're very busy. We're all so busy."

"Where is he? When can I see him? When can he come home?"

"Keep in mind, Arie was very sick."

"Was?" I felt suddenly weak. "Where is he?"

"I cared for Arie, too, Alison. You know how I felt about the two of you."

Gosford kept talking. He wasn't told, he said. He took my hands in his and squeezed. He said he didn't know. I didn't hear everything. Just the words, "Arie's gone." And once I heard them, I heard them again, over and over, increasing in volume until they resounded in my head like the world cracked open.

CHAPTER 8

When I finally returned to my cold and empty house, I crawled into my bed and slept for what I guess was several days. How long I actually lay there, fleeing one nightmare into another, I can't say. It felt like years. It felt like forever. I cried until the skin around my eyes became raw and abraded. I cried until I had no more tears.

Mostly I dreamed of how Arie might have died. What was wrong with him? What sickness had it been? Had he been in pain, crying out for me? I wondered when and why they finally gave up on him. Had it been a sudden ending, or had he slipped into unconsciousness and then to nothing without a sound? Or was he fevered, thrashing, like he'd been in his bedroom that night. Was he by himself? And which would be worse—alone in some corner of the dreary infirmary, or surrounded by indifferent Agency medical technicians, taking note of his condition but unable or unwilling to comfort him?

And then what? What did they do with him when it was over? The prospect broke and re-broke my mother heart. I must have dreamed of every possibility, no matter how grisly.

But the final nightmare was more frightful than all the rest.

I dreamed that Arie was still alive.

I dreamed that he was still up in his bedroom, indexing his information, sorting the books and news magazines he'd gathered over the past year. I made him soup and when I opened the door to bring it to him, he looked up and smiled at me in the candlelight.

"Smells terrible," he said, grinning.

I laughed.

Setting the papers aside, he said, "Thanks, Mom. Oh, man, I'm starved. I think I'll quit. Head to bed."

In this dream the books and notes were not strewn in manic mounds like the nest of some mad librarian. And they weren't on the floor, either. Instead, they were stacked on tables and neatly ordered. There was a system to their arrangement. An authority, even.

When Arie was alive, he never could tell me exactly why we searched the abandoned houses, scavenging for news reports and computer disks and the journals of children. Or he never would tell me. But he seemed to know that we needed them, and I knew only that I believed him. Despite how much it scared me to search the houses, I knew that, for Arie, I needed to.

In this final nightmare, the purpose of the information was clearer, and I eventually understood that somehow it would save us all, make us happier.

And I dreamed that Arie could actually explain it to me, opening one notebook, then another, pointing, reading to me. Little by little, he taught me his system, showed me the secrets he'd unlocked. And when he set the last notebook aside, I knew that something incredible was about to happen to us.

Then the dream changed. I saw notebooks on fire, notebooks sodden and moldering, torn pages blowing like dross down a forlorn road. Arie's explanations, which had filled me with such hope, became raving gibberish. The orderly stacks of notebooks now stood in wretched towers that teetered, threatening to tumble and bury us. And in the ghastly lachrymose glow of the low-burning candle lights, when Arie lifted his gaze from his ragged haphazard papers, his face was twisted with hysteria.

Then the dream seated me outside the door of the infirmary again, the edges of the dark unfeeling structure vanishing into the sullen mist in all directions, as if that oppressive building was all that existed.

The rest of the dream I knew already. The rest was my new reality. My new, less-complicated reality.

I opened my eyes.

My journal was on the bedside table, as if beckoning me to record the dream, record it all. Write it down. I pushed it to the floor. There was no sense in writing down anything anymore. No sense in writing about Arie, about us together. Why would I want to remember any of this? It would only make things worse. And after the treatment—what would be the point of being reminded of such?

I rose from bed and went downstairs to sit in the big chair by the front window. The house was so quiet now. Through the window I watched the snow fall. First it covered the weeds and crumbling sidewalks. Then it buried the rotting cars. The temperature dropped. No one was seen outside. It kept snowing for three days.

In a few months, I'd go back to the infirmary and they'd put the needles in my arm. All of the horror of the last year wouldn't just disappear, it would be as though it never happened, as though this version of me never existed. Instead of a curse, I began to see it as a blessing. With a little extra paperwork and red tape, I could have my record amended to show that I'd never had a child at all. I wouldn't have to feel this pain. I could burn the journals beforehand—mine and Arie's. I could burn them as fuel to boil enough water for a long, hot bath, take the serum, and when I awoke on the other side, there would be no life or love to miss or mourn. For the first time in nine or ten months, I longed for the end of the year.

I longed to be erased.

There were times when I slept through the day and didn't so much as open my eyes until it was dark, which left me with the impression that the sun had stopped rising.

I had at least stopped crying.

One day I awoke in the chair by the front window and I looked outside. The sun shone through torn and broken clouds. The storm had almost cleared away. More than two feet of snow had accumulated. It lay undisturbed over everything like a vast covering of cake frosting.

A flock of pine siskins was attacking the fir tree across the street, prying the last of the seeds from its cones with their hard tiny beaks. They chased and scolded in the branches. On the snow around the tree lay a dusting of fir needles and seeds and cone scales. As more of the noisy little birds arrived to raid the fir, they knocked the snow loose from the boughs, and it fell in cascading, powdery waves to the ground, where it buried the ring of seeds and needles.

I heard a noise from the front porch. Someone had trudged up the snow-covered steps and was turning the doorknob. After finding the door locked, there was a soft knock.

It was Arie.

Of course it was. It had to be. It had all been a mistake. That happened sometimes—fouled-up records, wrongful arrests, collapsed memories. I'd heard of that happening many times. Someone might vanish and be gone for a few days, even weeks, before reappearing without explanation.

Arie had been put in the wrong bed, maybe.

Misidentified. Misdiagnosed. Maybe they'd held him for questioning—they'd found out about his contraband, his searches outside the Zone. It was some kind of mistake.

But now he was back.

I ripped my blanket away, scrambled from the chair, and pounded across the room to the door.

But it wasn't Arie. There'd been no mistake. It was two knocks followed by a pause and then a third knock.

"Alison. Hello."

"Oh. Hello, Gary." I stepped aside to let him into the house.

"Are you okay? You look—am I bothering you?"

"No, it's just—" I stammered and sighed. "I'm tired."

"You should probably be resting." Gary said. "I know it hasn't been easy."

I nodded.

Gary took a deep breath.

"Alison," he said, "I want you to know how sorry I am about what happened."

"I appreciate that."

"I'm devastated, Alison. Really. I'm so very sorry. I would have done anything to help him."

"But you couldn't," I said, realizing too late how much that must have sounded like an accusation.

"No," he said softly, his gaze falling to the floor.

He'd tracked snow into the living room. He watched it melt into the carpet. "I wasn't told. They didn't tell me. I didn't know."

"Then you have nothing to be sorry about."

"Yes, but, I feel like I need to make it up to you somehow. I can't bring him back, but please let me help you. Some way."

He took a step toward me. I could see from his face that he was sincerely troubled, hurt.

"You do help me, Gary. You helped us a lot. And I appreciate it."

"I want to do more for you than bringing you a little food or propane. You've lost your son. I know he was a hard worker. I know he helped a lot around here. And maybe you get lonely sometimes, like I do. Maybe you'd like some companionship."

All I wanted was to go back to bed.

"Could I come by and help you Alison? With anything you need around the house? Or just to talk?"

Maybe it would be nice to have someone around. To have company, at least. Someone to help.

I shrugged. "If you want."

"I do, Alison. It would mean so much to me."

Without Arie and his searches and our journals and adventures, I knew the tedium and strain of this life would grind me into sand. And I wanted to feel safe, if only until it was time to take the serum again. I wasn't sure I even knew what it was to feel like myself, but there were several months remaining. Something had to change.

Having an adult in my house—how would that be? Having someone I could speak with; someone I could trust—how different it would be. And Gary was someone with connections, a man who could help me with matters more grave than drafty windows or a broken-down bicycle.

Gary said he would be back in a couple days to help me work around the house. The windows really did need caulking and there were other chores. He might have even worn the hint of forlorn smile as he put his hat on and went out into the deep snow.

This made me slightly sorry for him—I longed for the new year now, and any kind of friendship we might cultivate would be wiped away in just a few months. Gary's offer brought me a faint hope, but he wasn't my way out. Instead, I felt the way I thought a patient of assisted suicide might feel—I was consigned. I would get through these last few months, and then I would embrace oblivion and escape from pain.

CHAPTER 9

The house had fallen into disarray—my clothing was strewn on the floor and over chair backs; cups and bowls lay discarded around the place. One day I stepped and slipped on my journal as I came into my bedroom. I must have been stepping on it or over it for a week or more, because the cover was spindled and partially detached. Something made me pick it up and take it with me to my chair by the window. As I thumbed through the pages, something in my mind began to change.

Arie would want me to remember him. I knew on some level that was true even as I had fought through blackest of my despair. Sitting in the chair and reading through my terse and lackluster entries in my journal, the truth gnawed at me. Arie wrote in his journals constantly, and he spent the rest of his spare time compiling what was basically a cross-referenced indexed history of the world we'd all forgotten. He'd want to be remembered, and he'd want me to write down everything else, too.

But this new realization concerned what *I* wanted, and what was good for *me*, as well as what Arie would want.

If I went to the infirmary at the end of the year and took my shots, I'd forget Arie—but only in a technical sense. His name, our past, and maybe even his face would be wiped from my mind, but was it that simple?

As soon as the Agency had told me that I had a son, back at the beginning of the year, I'd known it to be true.

The Agency worker had traced her gloved finger down her clipboard. "Your son, Arie, will be here shortly," she said to me.

"I'm sorry," I said. "My what now?"

"Your son," she said. "Yes. Arie. They're bringing him out now. Just take a seat."

"I have a—son?"

"You have a son."

In the months that followed, every time I finished one of Arie's sentences for him, or knew what he wanted to eat for dinner before he asked, I became more certain that we were mother and son.

And this was the problem.

Because if I had carried that certainty with me through the memory-erasing serum, I could never really forget Arie. If there were no one to remind me that I had a son, I would instead feel his absence in my life, his negative image, and I would carry the sadness of his passing without knowing why.

I went to kitchen, brewed a strong cup of tea, and ate several stale granola bars. Then I opened my journal to a new page and set it on the table in front of me. In the spiral binding there was a stubby pencil. I drew it out and sharpened it with my pocket knife.

Outside, the sunlight receded and then there was only cold starlight on the snow glowing dim and blue. The moon rose and still the siskins darted among the fir tree branches.

Without my journal, without a complete record, Arie really would cease to exist. It would be as if he had never existed. His name might appear in some inactive file or graves registry, but there would be no description of the way he ran his fingers through his bangs when they fell into his face, or how his nose scrunched when he laughed hard. At that moment, Arie existed only in my mind and nowhere else. I had to bring him out and write him down.

And so I threw away my lonely, desperate plan—crumpled it up and tossed it like a page of unsatisfactory writing from a notebook. I would take the serum, but I would also leave behind a record of Arie that I could keep beyond the scrim of forgetting. And it would be a good record, one I could keep regardless of whether we ever regained our memories.

At first I wasn't sure if I could do it. How could I when he was so recently gone? Wouldn't every page I wrote feel like losing him all over again? As I finished the last of my tea, I decided that it didn't matter—it was my pain, and I was keeping it. Besides, the hurt would fade with time, as all hurts do, but the love would stay vivid. I smoothed the fresh new page and began to write.

I'd mentioned Arie in my notebooks before, of course, but I'd never written much expressly about him, never even described what he looked like. I'd committed the very error Arie had warned me about—I wrote as a diarist, not a journalist. My entries assumed the future reader would know everything I knew in those moments: background, context, and history.

"Write to your future self, not your present self," said Arie. "Write like you're writing to a stranger, because that's what you'll be when you read this next year."

Now it made sense, and I wished I'd listened better. I'd written of Arie most when we were first re-united, immediately after our treatment at the first of the year. He'd conceived the journal-writing idea within the month, and I'd made a few notes back then. But the entries from that time were crude, cursory, as though I was still coming to grips with my responsibility to him. Not to mention I was still getting to know him, and I was enjoying our time together.

Later on, after I'd gotten accustomed to his constant presence in my life, he was mentioned even less—and less informatively. A stranger could learn little about him from my journal. I'd made too many assumptions, too many omissions.

I had to start over completely.

And so I scared up a new notebook and wrote through the night. My candle burned out as the sun rose on the drifted snow outside. The siskins merrily raided the fir tree in the cold. I kept on writing.

*

It took me almost three hours to reach Donna's RV.

By the time I'd used up all the notebooks we had in the house, an icy crust had formed on top of the snow, and my snow boots broke through it with practically every step. The drive-in theater parking lot was a series of soft undulations covered over by the glittering, white blanket. The cats were gone, and there were few tracks in the snow around the RV. However, a pipe on the roof emitted a stream of vapor that whipped in the breeze.

"Donna?" I shouted as I approached. "It's Alison."

Winter clothes weren't hard to come by, so I was dressed warmly, but I'd gotten sweaty and damp trudging for so long through the crusted drifts. The wind picked up and the sun was dropping and I shivered violently under my layers of fleece and Gortex. I rested awhile, made a few more post-holes through the snow toward the RV, and then I called to Donna again.

She didn't come to the door, and I saw no stirring

inside. I kept going until I stood thigh-deep in the snow at the base of the wooden steps.

"Donna!"

No response.

I stepped onto a lower stair and banged on the door with my gloved hand.

"Donna, please," I shouted. "Kinda cold out here."

I stood there a few minutes. She didn't come. If I didn't start back right away, I might freeze to death, so I unshouldered my backpack and drew open the heavy zipper. Inside there was a bundle of books held together with rubber bands.

"Donna, I've got books," I said. My voice halted and hitched with my shivering. I held the books up in case she was watching. "I'll leave them out here. But I really need more notebooks."

I banged on the door again. It stayed shut. The speaker masts of the drive-in theater stood in their rows across the lot, casting blue shadows that seemed to lengthen as I waited. I cleared a flat spot in the snow on the wooden steps and set the books there like some shabby, unwrapped Christmas gift. Then I stood to go, placing my boots in the post holes I'd left.

When I'd taken ten or twelve steps, as I'd hoped, I heard the door handle click.

"'Bout time, Donna," I whispered. Then I turned around.

The snow had piled up and froze in front of the door, and Donna had to put her weight behind it to push it open. She peeked out at me.

"Hi, Donna," I said, waving. I gestured at the snow with a gloved hand. "Hey, wow! How about this weather?"

She crouched at the door and picked up the books.

"I hope you like those," I said, pointing. "I know you like those classics, the brainy stuff."

She examined the spines, read the titles—*The Great Gatsby, Catch-22, One Flew Over the Cuckoo's Nest, Orpheus Descending.*

"Donna. It's awful cold out here. Any chance I could come in for a minute?"

She pulled one of the books from the bundle and took a close look and I saw the faint smile I'd seen before when she found a book she wanted. She nodded to me.

I climbed the staircase of hard snow as Donna got the door all the way open. Then I stepped into the RV. Donna backed into the dim interior as I entered. It was even more cluttered than it looked from outside. The books were everywhere, and the air was stuffy with their acrid, musty odor. Four or five cats appeared from under the stairs and slipped into the open RV, threading around and between my ankles. They climbed onto the piled books and sat monitoring me like Egyptian sentinels. Donna went to the couch by way of a narrow path that ran between the books. She sat down and then motioned with a stiff, awkward gesture for me to join her. I opened my coat and removed my hat and gloves. We sat a while without speaking.

"I was sorry to hear about your son," said Donna. Her voice had a muddy quality, as though she might be medicated. Her eyes were always slightly glassy, too. But who could medicate her? And why?

"You heard?"

She nodded.

"How?"

"You're not the only one who comes."

"Oh."

It was only marginally warmer inside the RV than it

was outside, but we were protected from the wind, and a handful of ruddy embers burned like a clutch of incandescent eggs in the belly of a tiny wood-gas stove in the corner. Already I was feeling the painful, itchy tingle of restored circulation in my fingers and toes. The cats blinked drowsily but kept their watch.

"You're here for notebooks?" asked Donna.

"Yes, please. And pens. Or pencils. Hell, crayons. I need to write."

"About Arie."

"Yeah," I said, my voice hitching. "I have to write down everything about him, or he'll be forgotten forever."

"There are no more notebooks," she said.

"What? Are you sure?"

"I'm sorry."

"No," I said. "I'm sorry to bother you. It's just—I need to write. I'm nowhere near finished."

"How much more is there?"

That was a question I'd been asking myself for days.

My hand throbbed with writer's cramp. My wrist was numb and stiff, and there were raw patches on the knuckles of my little finger where they rubbed the paper. I'd been writing for days, everything I could remember. I'd read all of Arie's journals, some of them more than once. I'd read his notes about his searching and collecting. I'd scoured my own journal, too.

The process had been chaotic, exhausting. I worked practically from the time I awoke, writing, reading, thinking, writing more. I could not stop at night until I collapsed. Sometimes I would awake with a start in the middle of the night with some newly remembered image or nuance, and I would light a candle and write it down. Each morning I would start again.

It had not been unpleasant. Alternating between grinning and crying as I strained to recall each day and moment with Arie—no, it wasn't unpleasant at all. As I read over what I'd written I'd laugh and cry some more.

There was the first day I met Arie at the Agency depot, and our long walk home, so awkward I thought I'd cry or maybe break down and giggle.

"What do you like to do?" I asked him.

He shot me a skeptical, sideways glance and then said, "How the hell should I know?"

We laughed, and things got better.

Then our first night as mom and son. It took us two hours to make one can of pork and beans because we couldn't find anything in the kitchen of our own assigned house.

"We need to reorganize this kitchen," I suggested. "Or else we're gonna starve."

Arie immediately pointed out: "That's probably what we did last year."

I wrote about the first neighborhood we searched and the way it seemed that Arie would never tell me everything he knew, or thought he knew. I wrote about the ideas he would share with me, especially when we talked all night.

"Do you really think it's an accident?" he once asked me. "Do you really think there was some plague, and the treatment just happens to wipe out our memories?"

"You mean you think it seems kind of—"

"Made up? Yeah. That's exactly what I think."

I wrote about my final day with him and waiting in vain for him to come out of the door at the infirmary.

There were some events and things that I'd written about already, but my writing had since become stronger, clearer, and more focused. The memories I wrote down again during that journaling marathon benefited greatly from my new perspective and ability.

In answer to Donna's question, I did not know how much there was to write down. I only knew there was more. With every memory and every line I put on the paper, two more would occur to me. But how to write it all? And when? How long would it take, and how would I know when I'd finished?

"There are a lot of blank pages in some of the journals," I said, more to myself than to Donna. "I could collect those, write small. Maybe write between the words of the used-up journals, in the margins. I can write on the pages of magazines and books."

"You know, Alison," she said. "There may be something that you're not thinking of."

"What do you mean?"

Donna looked around the RV, at her shelves of books. All at once she seemed to be under the influence of some spell. Her eyes were suddenly brighter and her voice clearer. And although my mind had gone fuzzy with worry and exhaustion, I came to attention. Even the cats seemed to await Donna's next utterance.

"Words on paper are—" she paused and blinked a few times, searching for the word. "Words on paper are ephemeral. They get lost. They burn."

"Okay," I said. "What are you trying to—"

"There is a time for writing," said Donna. She looked my way. Her eyes were wide behind her spectacles. "But sometimes to unlock the secrets, it's better to find the right book."

CHAPTER 10

Donna's cryptic pronunciation immediately brought to my mind the flowered diary I'd found hidden in the girl's bedroom that day the feral dogs had attacked us. It was like a cup of icy water had been dumped down my back. The secret journal that would have stayed hidden forever had Arie not admonished me to search carefully.

Donna began to talk about books. She tapped the paperback spine of *One Flew Over the Cuckoo's Nest* and said, "Ken Kesey faked his own death, you know."

"No, I didn't know that," I said.

Another journal.

She looked at me and blinked a few times. "Hemingway was bi-polar," she said, tapping her temple softly with the book. "Heard voices."

A hidden journal.

The cats left the room as if they'd been issued some cue. I couldn't tell where they'd gone.

A secret journal.

Donna continued. She cited facts about books and writers. She told me how texts of ancient scripture had been corrupted in translation, and even faked or encoded.

Arie had a secret journal. That's where he kept his real secrets.

I don't remember what excuse I gave Donna, but a few minutes later I fled her RV, and it took me half as long to get home. I ran up the stairs to Arie's bedroom without pausing to remove my coat or gloves.

I hadn't gone into his room very many times since that night; it was too hard not to picture him still there on the floor. Someone, maybe Gary or the neighbors across the street, had come in at some point and neatly piled the papers and books, but it didn't matter. I saw them there anyway, and Arie with them.

My mind keened at the prospect that there might be something of Arie yet to find, something he'd kept from me. I took off my coat and gloves and boots.

First, I reread all the notebooks and journals, looking for clues. So much writing, so many numbers. As the day brightened to afternoon and then faded to dusk, I read each one. Nothing. That night I sat on Arie's unmade bed, careful not to disturb the pillow, which I imagined still held an imprint from when he'd last laid his head there. My eyes wandered around the room. So many places Arie had always told me to check when we went through the abandoned houses—under the mattress, between the mattresses, behind furniture, beneath carpeting.

But those hiding places seemed too obvious for Arie, and in any case the last thing I wanted to do was ransack his room. Arie liked his things neatly arranged. I would never be able to get it back the way he'd placed them, and even the undisturbed space between his meager possessions was something I didn't want to lose.

The sunlight drained from the room, turning from dusk to night. Searching by candlelight would be slow and clumsy, but the curiosity was like a pointy rock in my shoe. Then again, I wondered whether I might spend hours in search of something I was simply hoping was there, but wasn't.

And so I stayed there on the bed for a long while, trying to see the room the way he would. There wasn't much in the room to search through, anyway. I saw his battered old basketball on the dresser. He'd hung a dartboard on the back of the door, but he never did find any darts. A collection of bike wheels and parts lay in one corner, along with his toolset. There was a shelf with a few books and the desk with his indexing and cross referencing, but I'd been all through those already. Arie would never hide something by simply placing it under or behind something. He was too paranoid. If Arie hid something, it'd be concealed. It'd be inside something that was inside something else, and maybe inside something else again. When it got too dark to see, I lay down on the bed and thought I might just sleep there. I realized then that the mattress was really quite shoddy, too soft in some spots and too hard in others, and I winced at the guilt of that. So like Arie not to complain. In the gloom I turned to lie facing the wall and somehow managed to fall into a dark, dreamless sleep.

I awoke with the dawn and the first thing I saw in the gathering light was Arie's dresser. Without thinking, I sat up, crossed the room, and searched the contents of every drawer. Then I checked each drawer for false bottoms. I found nothing. Next I turned to the bookcase. I thumbed through each book, set them aside, and rapped on the shelves and sides, searching for secret compartments like some spy in a movie. Still nothing. It occurred to me that if I had searched the empty houses this way, maybe we'd have found a library of real secrets. When I'd finished dismantling and inspecting the desk, I got on my belly and peered underneath everything. I felt my way along the carpet for something slipped underneath. On a frenzied whim, I pulled up the carpet altogether, ripping it from the tack strips, jerking it out from beneath the furniture. I flung it into the hallway.

"I'm sorry, son," I whispered. "I guess I'm ransacking after all."

On hands and knees, I examined the bare floor for loose boards, ran my hands along each section of molding. There was nothing. Maybe there was no journal, no secret. By this time, it was growing dark again, and so I lit a candle.

Only the bed remained. I checked between the mattresses, flipped the box spring upside down. Dust bunnies swirled on the floor around my feet. I held the candle so that I could see through the gauzy fabric and into the wooden ribs of the mattress box. As I did so, something small and hard shook loose from the bedding and fell to the floor. I picked it up.

It was a plastic action figure. A small, poseable man with a brown leather coat and fedora—an adventure hero from the movies. Arie was much too old for such toys, and I had never seen this one. It seemed likely that it was in the house before we lived there, but I knew instantly that it was Arie's, that he'd found it somewhere and kept it, and all at once I was reminded that despite his maturity and brilliance, he was a boy, too. He'd been my little boy. And he was gone.

"Alison, what are you doing?" A voice from behind me.

I screamed and flinched and spun around. Gary Gosford stood in the doorway staring at the disheveled room.

"Oh. Hi. I'm just—" My mind raced. The folds of pulled-up carpet, Aries things strewn around. The furniture askew.

"I knocked but nobody answered," said Gary. "I was worried. What happened here?"

My eyes rose to meet his. "I needed to—"

He stepped into the room and took the action man from me. "This was Arie's room?"

I nodded. He looked around the room slowly. He pressed his lips together.

"This is where you found him, then," he said in a soft voice. "Must be really hard to be in here."

"Hm? Oh. Yes. Yes. It is. Hard to come back. In here."

"I'm sure it'll get better, Alison. Try not to make yourself crazy," he said. He gestured at the room. "I'm not sure all of this is, you know, healthy." He stepped back, pocketing Arie's toy as he did. "Maybe try to keep busy with something else. Can you do that?"

All I wanted was for him to leave. "I'll try," I said.

"I can stay with you tonight, if you want."

"No, no," I said. "I'm fine. And actually, I'm feeling kind of tired now. I should go to bed."

"You're sure you're okay?"

"Yes, I'm feeling better. Thank you."

Gary looked around the room once more and shook his head. "I'll come by more often. Don't worry," he said.

When I was sure he had gone, I blew out the candles and lay down on the mattress to cry awhile—for Arie and his boyhood and for the hidden diary I couldn't find and probably didn't exist. For all my lost memories. I thought maybe I'd sleep there again, and so I kicked off my shoes and pants and groped in the dark to pull Arie's blankets around me. Again, that crummy mattress, that unevenness.

An unevenness that tattled on itself.

My heart thumped a few times. I rose up and patted the mattress. Something flat, rectangular, firm.

A notebook. It had to be.

Not under the bed, not between the mattresses, not even up in the space beneath the box spring, but inside the mattress.

"You sneaky little shit," I muttered.

I threw off the sheet and blanket and in the darkness I felt along the sides and seams of the mattress—yes, there at the top was a neat incision, no wider than necessary to admit a notebook. I reached in, chuckling that I'd been sitting on it when I first came in. I lit the candle once more.

It was an ordinary notebook, like the others we used. This one had a red cover, on which Arie had scrawled the outline of a human skull. Within the round space of the cranium, he'd drawn a clock face that indicated three o'clock. He'd traced it repeatedly with a ballpoint pen, for the lines were deeply incised into the heavy paper cover. And then he'd burnished the lines with a pencil eraser, so that it stood out in white.

I'd read all of Arie's journals—the first one began in January and the last one contained an entry from the day he collapsed. But I'd never seen this one. He must have felt he had to keep it secret, even from me. What if he wouldn't want me to read it? Even now that he was gone?

I ran a palm across the notebook's cover and the clock-skull figure. I sat there with the journal in my lap for several minutes, afraid to read what might be Arie's most intimate feelings. Afraid that releasing them, hearing them in my mind would mean that Arie would really be gone then.

With trembling hands, I took a deep breath and opened the notebook.

I scanned the first page and a gasp might have escaped me. Then I stood and turned the page. Row upon row of Arie's neat, smooth handwriting. I sat back down and flipped through all the pages. Every page was practically alike, and I wasn't sure whether to laugh or cry.

CHAPTER 11

The parking lot stretched for what seemed like a mile in all directions. In the distance, the Ferris wheel towered over the amusement park, which sat decaying and inert.

"Sky Dreamer," I whispered.

There was no evidence that anyone else was there or had been there recently. Most of the snow had vanished under two days of sunlight, but in the drifts and grainy patches that remained I saw no footprints, no bicycle tracks.

I drew a deep breath, took another look around, and started across the weedy expanse of pavement. Ravens and magpies atop the lamp poles tipped their heads to watch me cross below them. In the islands of melting snow, dry bleached stalks of weeds stood dead and trembling in the wind. The parking lot had begun to assume the appearance of a wild winter plain, and it was difficult to imagine that it had ever been filled with cars or the shimmering asphalt heat of summertime.

At last I reached the park entrance and stood beneath the arch which in faded and peeling letters welcomed visitors to Thrill Harbor. I turned to face the weedy pavement I'd crossed. Families would hurry in from their cars and minivans, converging here and passing excitedly through the turnstiles and on into the park. Now the place lay dead, a rotting checkerboard of melting snow and cracked tarmac. There were aluminum shutters drawn over the ticket windows and a cage-like barricade chained up and padlocked outside the turnstiles.

Some of the barricades had been partially pulled down, and so I clambered over them and then hopped over a bank of locked-down turnstiles. I thought of my dream and the man who took my ticket as the rides spun and strobed in the dusk, and that made me look up at the Sky Dreamer. There it was, arching into the empty sky above the buildings and lesser amusements.

Among the rides and shops it was shaded and cooler, and so I zipped the collar of my coat higher.

When Arie and I searched the neighborhoods, there had been a constant impression of not belonging in the vacant houses, the guilt of trespassers in a burial ground. But something was different here. Something or someone was hiding here. Lurking. I folded my arms.

The earth was even more enthusiastic about reclaiming the interior of park than the parking lot. Thick vines of bindweed and wild grape, now brown but nevertheless thick and sinewy, snaked up the walls and railings. Dead vines hung from the rides and power lines. On the roofs of the restrooms and concessions stands, black moss grew along the eaves, and wild maples and willows had taken root in the rain gutters. Shrubs had burst out of their landscaping beds and invaded the pavement thoroughfares. The grassy lawns were tall and dead, shoulder-high in some places along the margins of the midway.

A pillow of snow lay in each seat of the flying swing, and dirt-speckled snowdrifts were banked up on the sidewalks. The elements had exacted their price, flaking the paint and fading the plastic until all the colors merged to a kind of indeterminate gray.

Where to start? A sere breeze gusted down the midway, snatching my hair from beneath the hood of my coat. I tucked it behind my ear. So many buildings—gift shop, candy store, fun house—some burned, some collapsed. There were piles of debris and the occasional dead truck resting on deflated tires. So many places someone could hole up; so many places where someone might hide. I felt eyes watching me from every busted-out window and gaping doorway. Goosebumps rose on my neck and arms, and I wondered suddenly why I hadn't given a second thought to coming alone to find Ruby. I chewed my lip and went on.

I followed the midway and came to a grand carousel with fiberglass horses and hippogriffs skewered on masts striped with what must have once been gold and royal blue. Vines and woody weeds were growing up around bottom edge, and more vegetation had sprouted from the pipes of the calliope.

Beyond the carousel rose the Sky Dreamer, dark and tall against its backdrop of day. The midway continued into a broad tunnel that ran completely under the Ferris wheel and into the far half of the park. The wild grapevine grew thick and gnarly around the tunnel's gaping entranceway, giving it the appearance of a portal into some subterranean world. Water pooled down in the floor of the tunnel and formed a frozen pond of black mud that splintered and crunched underfoot. In the half-light I saw names and symbols and rude words scrawled on the walls.

In one place, someone had scrawled *Please Remember Me.*

Along one side of the tunnel, there was a line of red letters two or three feet high. There wasn't much light, but the writing stood out from the grime and older deposits of graffiti. In the darkness I could clearly make out the words: *BOATS AGAINST THE CURRENT BORNE BACK.*

The muddy water was deepest in the dark center of tunnel, where its drainage had no doubt been choked by garbage and sediment.

As I sloshed along, worrying that the filthy water might over-top my boots, I became all at once aware that I was not alone.

I glanced up, and there where the shadows were deepest, I thought I saw the silhouette of a man leaning against the wall of the tunnel near the far end.

I stopped short and held my breath. Then I couldn't see him. I cocked my head to one side and squinted.

I swallowed hard and said, "Someone there?"

The figure pushed off from the wall. "Who wants to know?" he asked.

A lanky, greasy-looking man unveiled himself from the dark and came my way through the muck.

I stepped back. My hands curled into fists.

As if the man's mere presence in the dank tunnel were not enough to make me recoil, as he came closer, I saw that his face was scarred by a livid gash that ran from his forehead, down through one eyebrow, and into the unkempt scraggle of his beard.

In his bony fist he held a bowie knife.

All my energy was building inside me to run. I felt like a compressed spring ready to release. But then I pictured myself running through the unfamiliar and tangled maze of the park, with its snow banks and walkways blocked by weeds and debris. I imagined the man giving chase. He probably knew the place better. He could probably run faster than me. And what if he had accomplices?

In the firmest, steadiest voice I could manage, I said, "Stay back."

"You shouldn't be here," he said.

"You stay back."

"What're you doing here?"

"None of your business," I said.

"Well, it is now."

He came forward, covering the distance between us in three or four quick strides. I swung my fist at him but he deflected it without much effort. Then he grabbed my coat and brought me to heel as though I were a misbehaving child. I tried to pull myself free of him, but the grip of his hand was like some great iron clamp. He pressed me against the wall and showed me the knife.

"Quit fightin'," he said. "You're comin' with me."

He kept the scruff of my coat in his balled fist and dragged me from the tunnel. I stutter-stepped and staggered along behind. I tried fighting him, but he kept me off-balance and tripping.

We came out of the tunnel on the other side of the Ferris wheel. The man towed me along a pathway that ran behind the rides and down a flight of concrete steps.

"Let go!" I hollered at him. "Where are you taking me?"

He gave me another jerk, harsh enough to hurt my shoulder. He was tall and strong. "Shut your mouth."

We approached what appeared to be the rear entrance of a low-slung brick building. Between two dumpsters there was a single metal door. The man looked around as if to ensure that no one was watching, and then pounded deliberately three times on the door.

It opened and another man stepped partway out. He was short and mostly bald with a big black beard.

"Who's this?" he said.

"Just get her inside," said the other.

The bald man did as he was told, and they dragged me in. My legs turned to water then, and I collapsed sobbing. I kicked and swatted at them. It had little effect.

CHAPTER 12

They tried dragging me deeper into the building but I screamed and caught hold of the door jamb. The tall one plucked my hands from the door and the short one got my legs. They wrangled me inside and shut the door. Then the only light to see by was that which filtered in from the small, high windows, but I know I saw a human skull impaled on a spear. Then another. Then a line of them, like a fence.

I twisted hard and they dropped me and so I thrashed and thrashed. They picked me up again, but my foot connected with someone's groin.

"Ow, Jesus, fuck," the bearded one squawked. "Glen, hold up. Chica just nailed me in the cajones, man."

They dropped me, but the one called Glen stepped on me and leaned forward until his weight compressed my ribcage. The other one bent over and steadied himself, his hand on the wall. He blew hard through his pursed lips as he reached down between his legs and gingerly readjusted himself.

"Glen, man," he said between gasps. "Who is this, anyways?"

"Caught her sneaking around up by the tunnel," said Glen jerking his chin.

"Well, chill for a second, will ya? I think she thinks we're gonna rape her."

Glen snorted and took his foot off me. He crouched down and jabbed at my face with his finger. "You're the one who was snooping around. I got a wife."

The bearded man knelt beside me. "Chica," he said. "You don't look like no spy. Who are you?"

"Who are you?" I spat back.

He stood up and ran a hand over his bald head.

"Well. Fair enough. I'm Carlos." He touched his chest with his palm. "This is Glen. He got a temper, but don't be a'scared of him. Now. Who are you?"

"I'm looking for someone," I said.

"That's not really what I asked, but, okay," said Carlos. "Who?"

"You wouldn't know her. Now let me leave."

Carlos shook his head slowly. "We need to know why you was out here."

"I told you. I'm looking for someone."

Glen lunged at me and bellowed, "Who!"

Carlos got between us.

"Her name's Ruby," I blurted. "She told me to come."

Their eyes widened, and the two of them traded a hard look. Glen licked his lips.

"Jesus, Chica," said Carlos. "Why didn't you just say so?"

He grabbed my arm and helped me to my feet. We continued down the darkened corridor, Glen leading the way and Carlos behind me. There were a number of dark corners. I couldn't say how many. Then we descended a roughly built wooden staircase into a tube-shaped brick passageway lit from above by a string of gloomy yellow utility lights. Along the way I saw alcoves to either side where shadowy figures lurked, frozen in menacing poses. In one alcove there was what had to be a mannequin zombie. In another, I saw a coven of motionless witches.

"Haunted house," I said quietly.

"Yeah," whispered Carlos. "The old haunted house ride. Creepy down here, huh? I hate it."

"Shut up and keep walking," said Glen over his shoulder.

We passed by a vampire figure whose grotesque store-bought rubber mask was half-obscured by a shroud of real cobwebs. There was a lady mannequin who'd been hacked in two by an ax murderer, her papier-mâché entrails dusty and desiccated.

Then I heard voices ahead. The passageway turned a corner and there in the bend was an opening blocked by a black velvet drape. Carlos parted the drape and I spotted Ruby in the small room beyond.

She was practically a stranger to me, a woman I'd met only a couple times, briefly, and yet I laughed suddenly at the sight of her.

It was a small concrete room with a single light bulb hanging from the ceiling. A workroom of some sort, adjacent to the ride. Dim light bulbs shown here and there, bathing the place with the dusky luster of a conspirator's lair.

Somewhere out of sight an electric generator hummed. Ruby leaned over a table, examining a large map through her bifocals. There was a candle burning at the center of the table, and when I looked closer, I could see that the map was actually a set of building plans. Ruby looked up and wrinkled her nose to reposition the spectacles. When she spotted me with my face red and hair wild, she straightened up and dropped her arms to her sides.

"Glen, what in Sam Hill is this?" she shouted.

Glen scratched the back of his neck.

"Well?"

"She was wandering around outside," he muttered.

Next to Ruby there stood a stout man with a round boyish face fringed with curly blond whiskers. He regarded me with a cool, Zen gaze. Behind them on the floor there was a coarse pallet and a man was lying on it, his head pillowed by a leather jacket. He had one arm thrown across his face, but he wasn't sleeping. Nobody could have slept through Ruby's tirade.

"Well, a'course she was," Ruby squawked, throwing up her arms. "I told her t'come!" Ruby's honking voice reverberated harshly in the small room and Glen recoiled as if bombarded by a hail of needles. Ruby scowled at him. If he'd been closer, she probably would have smacked him.

She limped over to me. "Actually, sis, you're lucky Glen found you. We've got the front entrance wired with explosives that'd blow ya here t'kingdom come."

"Oh my God, why would you do that?" I asked.

"To keep out unwanted guests," answered Ruby, as though the answer was obvious.

"But what about the new year? No one will remember."

"That's just it, sweetheart. This time I don't intend to forget," Ruby answered, tapping her forehead with a finger.

"She kicked Carlos square in the nuts," Glen tattled quietly, tilting his head at his companion.

"Yeah, but that was totally my bad," said Carlos. He waved a dismissive hand, but then he touched himself down there and winced a little.

"Alison, are you all right?" asked Ruby.

I nodded and joined her at the table.

"So. What's she here for?" Glen asked warily.

"She's got twice as much brains as you do, for starters." She turned to me again, jabbed her thumb at the stout fellow and said, "This here's Woolly."

Woolly was wider than two of me, maybe three. His arms were slab-like and his legs were thick as tree trunks, but his eyes were bright and thoughtful. He wore a black t-shirt and baggy denim shorts.

I nodded and he nodded back, closing his eyes and bowing ever so slightly.

Ruby gestured at Carlos and Glen. "These two knuckleheads y'already met."

They nodded and murmured diffident hellos.

"Everybody, this is Alison. She's a friend I made. A good egg. And smart." She rubbed my back and winked at me. "Had a feeling you'd come."

From behind Woolly stepped a young girl with curly blond hair and dirty cheeks.

"Hey, I know you," I said.

The girl looked up at me shyly. "You're his mom," she said. "The tall boy. He died, huh?"

"Gracie, shush," said Ruby, nudging the girl. Then Ruby turned to me and in a low voice said, "We heard about your boy. Awful sorry 'bout that."

"He used to give me apples," said the little girl in a soft voice. "But then he stopped."

"This here is Gracie," said Ruby.

It'd been a while since I'd thought about the wraith-like little girl Arie had fed from our back porch like a stray cat. Neither of us had ever known her name. Gracie acted as though she knew me, and I wondered how much she'd watched us and our house. The motherly part in me wanted all at once to pick her up and take care of her.

Not just because of her cherubic face and sweetness, but because she was a link to Arie.

"So, you're here to help, ain'tcha, honey?" Ruby asked me.

"Actually," I said, unshouldering the backpack, "I can't stay. I just wanted to ask you something. See, my son kept this journal. You remember? We both wrote in journals."

Ruby nodded, her brow furrowing.

I unzipped my pack and fished out Arie's secret red notebook. "I found one that Arie wrote, and I can't understand it."

Ruby frowned and shot me a quizzical expression. She took the notebook from me and perched herself atop a stool by the table. She adjusted her glasses and flipped through the pages awhile. Gracie peered over Ruby's arm.

It was only lines and lines of numbers. *55, 8, 12, 102, 10, 2.*

Pages and pages like that. Nearly the whole notebook. Ruby scanned the notebook, then regarded me over the top of her glasses.

"Is this all ya come for?" she asked.

"I need to know what it means," I said. "You seemed to know—things. What do you think this means?"

The others crowded close and leaned in to see. Somebody slid the candle closer.

"Was this kid on drugs?" asked Carlos.

Ruby socked him on the shoulder. "Idiot," she hissed.

He rubbed his arm.

Ruby removed her glasses. "The question you should be asking is why would he be needing to write in code."

"Is that what it is? Can you read it?"

"No," said Woolly, shifting heavily. "No one can." His voice was deep and coarse, but he had clear, refined diction. "Not without the key."

"Key?" I asked.

"Every code has a key," he said gently. He grabbed the waistband of his shorts and tugged them up, but they drooped again.

I looked at the journal. "So, how do I figure out what it says?"

"You don't," he said. "I'm sorry to break it to you this way, but that's the whole point. He'd have to give you the key. Or you'd have to find it yourself. Whoever wrote this—your son?"

I nodded hastily.

"Your son used a key to encrypt his words into these numbers." He tapped the journal with his finger, which was nearly as thick as my wrist. "Each number is a letter or a word. So, his words are all there, but they're hidden, locked. Find the key, unlock the words."

"What would the key look like?"

"Like a codebook. Or any ordinary book. Or just a chart. Depends on what he decided to use."

Ruby passed the journal to Woolly.

"I could study it a little," said Woolly, flipping the pages of the notebook with his thumb. "Then I could maybe tell you at least what kind of cipher it is. Wouldn't help you decrypt it, but it might make it easier to figure out what he used as a key."

"You would?" I said, "Oh, thank you."

"Now, hold on," said Ruby. "Woolly, you got plenty to do right now."

Woolly nodded and gave the notebook back to me. "She's right. I'm sorry. Maybe another time."

"Alison, I'm real sorry, too," said Ruby, "but we're

sort of in the middle of something here. Fact, I was hoping you could help us."

I stared at Arie's journal. There comes a moment when you think your pain couldn't possibly be worse. That you've reached an end to it. Like when Gary told me about Arie. I thought that was the bottom. But then you discover that pain can exist in deep, hidden pockets. Unexpected blooms of misery that appear suddenly, and you begin to wonder if there is a limit to how much you can hurt, or if eventually it will just kill you. What was in the journal? Was it a secret Arie had carried all year? Was it Arie himself?

I didn't plan to hurt myself, not with the new year so close, but I saw death in a new way after that: a sweet release. I was surprised by how often I thought about it after that. If I didn't keep myself distracted—didn't stay busy—that's where my mind would go.

"I understand," I said finally. "Thanks for your help."

I turned my face as I went so that they couldn't read my expression. Then I shoved the notebook in my bag and headed for the doorway and the black drape.

"Glen, show her how to get back out," said Ruby.

Glen had lit a pipe and there was the sweet odor of leaf tobacco in the air. He joined me at the doorway.

"Hey," Ruby called to me.

I stopped.

"You never seen his body, didja?" she asked.

I turned around. "What?"

"Your kid. J'ever see him? After, I mean. Not to be mean, but, didja?"

I shook my head.

"Didn't think so."

"Why?"

"Look. I'm not saying he's alive," Ruby said. "I'm just saying if you didn't see his body, how do you know he's really dead?"

"Why would they tell me that?" I asked.

"Why would he be writin' in a code?" Ruby asked.

The man on the floor sat up and sighed. "When they can control your memories, they control everything."

"Chase, get up. Come help figure this out," Ruby said, rotating the blueprint one way, then another. "It's gonna be the new year and I'll still be standing here try'na read this here floor plan."

The man rose stiffly and joined her at the table. He was tall and fit, but his clothing was disheveled and he wore a three-day beard.

"Chase, that there's Alison. Alison, this here's Chase."

He shrugged at me, as if he had no choice but to admit his identity.

"Help me with this, Chay," said Ruby.

"Floor plans?" he asked while tousling Gracie's hair. "How'd you get these?"

"From my contact," said Woolly. "If we can crack into this base, we might be able to figure out where they keep this uncut serum—if it exists. Maybe we find a lot of stuff."

"If Arie's alive," I interrupted, "then where would he be? How can I find him?"

Ruby sighed and pressed her lips together. "Listen, sweetie, I feel for ya. But we've got things here that can't wait."

"Neither can I," I said. "It's almost the new year. If I don't find out now, I never will. Please. He's all I have."

They all stared at me for a few moments.

Ruby pulled the glasses off her face and chewed the

inside of her cheek. "We could use a hand here," she tapped the plans with the folded-up glasses. "Maybe we can help each other."

"Okay," I said. "What can I do?"

"I don't know," said Ruby chuckling. "What can you do?"

"Let's table this for now," said Chase. He stretched and scratched himself sleepily. "Let's focus. If that serum is sitting somewhere, then let's go get it."

They seemed to forget I was in the room.

"Can't," said Ruby. "We don't know exactly where it's at. There's six, eight buildings here. Big ones. And these plans're old. Serum could be anywhere. And there's fences. Guards. Locks. God, this is a big problem." She indicated the plans with a nod. "So. Where's it gonna be?"

Chase scratched his whiskers and grimaced. "All right. There's gonna be an office. This much storage space, there'll be records, you know, manifests. Probably on a computer. A database. Or maybe just a spreadsheet. We have to start there."

Woolly nodded.

They bent over the table and scanned the plans. I took a step forward, but none of it made any sense to me. I'd crossed the Zone boundaries countless times with Arie, but these people were planning to break in and steal things—directly from the Agency, it seemed. Serum? Why steal it? The Agency was going to give it to all of them whether they wanted it or not. Just thinking about what would happen if we were caught talking about these things made my mouth dry.

"There must be fifteen offices here," said Woolly. "One here. A couple here. Most of these warehouses have office space. We could spend an hour just trying to find the right one."

"Yeah," said Chase. "We'll never find it staring at twenty-year-old blueprints."

"Then how?" said Ruby.

They all stood motionless for a while.

"Electricity," said Woolly.

"Ah," said Chase, nodding. "Right."

"Whaddya mean?" asked Ruby.

"They can't power the whole site," said Woolly. "They can barely supply power at all. We just need to figure out which building has power, lights. That's where the computer will be."

"Woolly," said Ruby, "go figure that out today. Take Carlos."

Woolly nodded.

"Alls we need now is a vehicle to get it out of there. Chase, didja find us somethin'?"

"Of course I did," he said. "And it's a truck. But."

"Why am I not surprised," Ruby said. "*But* what?"

"It's a manual transmission," Chase said.

"So?"

"I—can't drive a stick."

"You kidding me?" she said.

"I guess I never learned. Or maybe I've forgotten how. I tried. Nearly dropped the tranny. I suppose I could try again, practice. But right now, I really can't. Can you?"

"Well. No."

"Me neither," said Carlos.

"I can," I said.

"Woolly," said Ruby. "Tell me you can."

"Sorry, Boss. I'm thinking I was more of a public transit sort of guy."

"Glen," said Ruby, her tone acid. "I know you can

barely find your ass with both hands, but I don't suppose—"

He shook his head. "Nope. Back to square one. Maybe we should spend our last days on earth enjoying life."

"Ruby," I said, my voice raised. "Hey. I can drive a stick."

They turned their heads in unison to face me.

"Rube," said Chase, jabbing his thumb at me, "who is she again?"

"Chase," said Ruby, "shush."

"I mean, I think I can," I said. "I don't actually remember ever driving one, but you just step on the clutch, put it in gear, then let off the clutch and step on the gas—right?" I did an awkward pantomime.

Ruby put both hands on the table. "Alison, this is really important. Do ya really think ya can?"

"Yeah. I do. When do we leave?"

She grinned, watching me over her eyeglasses. "We'll have Chase take you to the truck and see what you can do. But first, there's something we need to take care of."

They all looked at me. Why were they all looking at me?

"What?" I said.

"You got a tracker," said Ruby.

"My chip? What about it?"

They kept staring at me. No one speaking.

I put my hand to the back of my neck.

"You mean you're chip-rippers? No. You can't take my chip. I won't be able to get rations without it. They'll think I'm a criminal."

Ruby sighed. "Listen Al, are you in or not?"

I'd read something once in a book about Maslow's Hierarchy of Needs. About how a person's physiological and safety needs took precedence before social needs like family and love. But at the moment, I suddenly realized I didn't actually care about where I'd find food to eat or live or get medical care. I didn't care that involving myself with this group would put me at odds with the Agency. I only wanted one thing—Arie. I wasn't sure if there was any chance that he was still alive, but at that instant I'd have given up everything to find out.

I fingered the slightly raised area of scar tissue on my neck.

"I'm in," I said.

CHAPTER 13

Around five miles from Thrill Harbor, on a remote dirt road far from any buildings, there was an old maroon Toyota Tacoma parked in the middle of the highway. It had big, off-road tires, and the back window was spangled with stickers from Moab and Yosemite and other places. The truck's body was caked in dust and the paint was sunburned and hazy, but the tires were full and hood was still shut—both signs that it might start and drive.

"Here you go." Chase tossed me the keys and then headed for the passenger seat.

The suspension was lifted six or eight inches. I wasn't even sure at first how to get in. I tried stepping up with the wrong foot, but it was too high. Then I grabbed at the steering wheel.

Chase opened the passenger-side door, took hold of a grab handle on the door frame and hoisted himself in.

"Need help?" Chase asked, but in a tone that made me know he wasn't really offering.

"No, I got it," I said. I grabbed the handle the way he had and pulled myself up.

Chase watched me skeptically.

You could tell he was smart. The way he spoke, the

way he figured things out. There was no good explanation why someone like him couldn't drive a stick-shift, but there were cases of unexplained specific forgetfulness. I knew I had been a mother and probably a wife before the virus, but I couldn't seem to remember how to make cookies or bread or cake. Had I known but forgotten with the serum, or had I never learned? I might not ever know.

Chase was handsome, or maybe it was just that he was rugged—his hair was auburn and he looked good in a beard. Despite his roughness, there was a time when I would have wanted to get to know him better, see if there was any chemistry between us, but that part of me seemed to have died with Arie. Not that any of it would have mattered. In a little over two months, we wouldn't remember each other, anyway.

I pulled the door shut. There was a stale smell inside. The steering wheel felt grimy. It looked like the windshield hadn't been wiped in years.

"Where'd you get this? Doesn't seem to be a lot of cars that actually work anymore."

"I know how to get stuff."

"I see."

"So, what's your story? Lost your kid? How old was he?"

"I don't want to talk about that," I said.

"Oh. Good."

I shot him a frown.

"'Cause neither do I," he said with shrug.

I pulled out my seatbelt and as I turned my head to find the latch, the seatbelt rubbed against the bandage on my neck where Chase had removed my Agency chip. It'd hurt more than I expected to have it removed and the skin was still tender. After they removed it, I had second thoughts about destroying it, but before I could say anything, the gang had already stomped it into a tiny pile of glassy dust.

Chase didn't buckle up.

I put the key in the ignition, tightened my ponytail, and adjusted the rear-view mirror. Then I examined the instrument panel and controls—out of some reflexive impulse, I suppose. I wouldn't really need blinkers or wipers or the radio, but I wanted to know where the knobs and levers were, nonetheless.

When you've lost your memories, you can't always trust the things you think you know because you don't know where they came from. Had I really ever driven a car with a manual transmission? Who had taught me that skill? Someone presumably had, but there was no reason to know for sure until I gave it a try.

"We won't drive too far," Chase said. "Can't waste gas. Just enough to see what you've got."

"Okay." I took a deep breath. "Let's go."

I stepped on the clutch and turned the key. The engine rumbled to life. It had a deep, throaty idle. Definitely a guy's truck. So far, so good. I took the shift lever in my hand and waggled it—to ensure it was in neutral. Who had taught me that? Where had I seen it? As surely as someone had taught me to walk, someone had taught me how to put a car in gear. With a foot on the brake, I depressed the clutch and shifted into first. Then I took my foot off the brake and pressed down on the gas pedal with my toe, but I released the clutch too quickly, and the truck lurched forward violently and stalled so abruptly we were launched into the seat belts.

"Jesus," snapped Chase. "I knew it."

"Hang on. I'm trying, okay? Maybe you oughta put your seatbelt on."

Chase rubbed his forehead. "This isn't gonna work."

"Give me a chance," I said. "Who knows how long it's been since I drove. And it's my first time in this truck. That I know of."

"We don't have time for you to learn how to drive all over again," he said.

"Well then we definitely wouldn't have time for you to learn," I shot back.

"Touchy."

"Would you shut up and let me do this?"

Chase folded his arms and slumped in his seat.

My hands had gone sweaty, making the large steering wheel slippery. I exhaled and turned the key again, but it wouldn't start.

"Now what?" said Chase.

"I don't know. Oh. The clutch."

With the clutch in, I started the truck again. I put it in gear, released the clutch, and applied the gas.

"Come on," I muttered.

The truck jerked again, nearly stalling, but then it rolled ahead.

"Yes! Yes, I did it!"

I looked over and caught Chase rolling his eyes. He clapped his hands silently with a patronizing grin on his face.

As the truck gained speed, the engine revved beneath the hood.

"You need to shift," said Chase, raising his voice over the noise. "Even I know that."

"I know. I know."

I shifted into second and we put on more speed. The packed-earth road was one of the few I'd seen that wasn't obstructed by old cars.

"See?" I said. "No problem."

"Yeah, yeah." Chase made a half-hearted effort to sit up in his seat. "I wouldn't call it a stellar performance, but we don't have a lot of options."

"I'd like to see you do better," I said.

"Turn here."

I downshifted and slowed. It was coming back to me.

"I don't know where you're planning to go. Most of the roads are blocked or broken up," I said.

"Drive into the field." Chase pointed. "The ground's frozen. We'll go this way tomorrow."

I steered into an old farm field grown wild with grass, and the truck squeaked and groaned as it bounced over the uneven ground.

"So, what is this top-secret mission, anyway?" I asked.

"Gotta pick something up."

"Pick up?" I turned to him. "You mean steal, right?"

"Don't sweat it," he shrugged. "Should be pretty basic."

We drove around for a while, and even with Chase's sarcastic remarks, it was kind of fun. It felt almost carefree. I even did a donut in the dirt. Then we parked the truck and walked back to Thrill Harbor. Chase set a time to meet early the next morning, offered up a terse "thank you" and "good night," and then I biked toward home.

The sun had almost completely set by the time I got to my house. The birds had quieted; the street was empty. I chained up my bike at the side of the house. Arie's bike was still there—one of thousands of painful reminders I encountered throughout the day that reminded me he was gone.

I was worn out for a change and eager to sleep. For weeks I had simply drifted in and out of a nonspecific state of feverish torpor. Writing the journals, reading them, sleeping and eating whenever. But that night I felt like I'd been productive in some new way, and I looked forward to lying down in bed for a restful night's sleep. Or was I just eager for morning? For the first time in a long time, I had something besides notebooks and pencils to wake up for.

I was taking off my coat by the front door when I thought I heard something in the house. I paused, but heard nothing. But as I hung my things on the coat rack, it came again—the creak of a floor, the feeling of an unseen presence. The house was dark. I looked into the living room and in the shadows, I thought I could see someone sitting there.

"Alison," Gary said.

As my eyes began to adjust to the darkness, he rose from the couch and slipped something beneath his long wool coat. A gun?

"My God," he said. "I thought you were dead."

"Dead? Why would you think that?"

He gave me a big hug and sighed.

"Don't you know I keep an eye on you? With everything that's happened and you being on your own—there's a lot of danger out there."

"I don't understand."

He tapped the back of his neck. "Your chip," he said. "It's off. I couldn't ping you. What's going on? What happened to you?"

"Oh, right. That. Yes. It's gone," I said. "They ripped it out."

"Who ripped it out?" cried Gary. "Who's 'they'?"

"I don't know, Gary. I don't know who they are. I was visiting some friends and as I was coming home someone attacked me."

"Good God, Alison. Are you hurt? Let me see."

"Was that a gun? Do you have a gun?"

"Yes. I carry one at times. I thought something might have happened to you—had to be ready if someone came to loot your place. Now what happened here?"

He leaned in to see my neck. I went to the kitchen to light a lantern.

"I slapped a dressing on it," I said. "It hurts a little. Why would someone do this, Gary? Why would they attack me?"

"There are some individuals—outside the Zones, mostly," he said. "They remove their own chips but steal others to get supplies. I'll see that they're found. Are you all right?"

"I think so. They held me down. It was over quick and then they took off. It just stings."

In the harsh lamp light, Gary examined the dressing, lifted it.

"This doesn't look too bad. Not too much damage, anyway. Thank God."

"Yeah, I think I'll be okay."

"Let's get you down to the infirmary right away. They'll install a new one. It happens. I'll submit an incident report. They won't question you that way. Your account is flagged, so as soon as someone tries to use your chip, they're screwed."

"Thanks. I'll go first thing tomorrow."

He frowned. "Straight in tomorrow, okay? You don't want to get caught without your chip. It's too risky."

"Yeah," I said. "I know."

CHAPTER 14

It had been awhile since I'd been awake and up so early before the dawn. I couldn't remember when, but it would have been with Arie. Sometimes when he wanted to search somewhere far from the house, we'd rise early and make breakfast in the dark. We'd pack up food and water for the day and go out and sit on our bikes to wait for enough light for riding.

How imperceptible the moment when darkness crosses into dawn and then from dawn into day, and yet how irrefutable. You can say it's day only when it's no longer night.

I found Chase already waiting for me in the dark by the Toyota. He was eating wild sunflower seeds from his pocket and spitting the husks on the ground.

"Why so early? Won't even be light for another hour."

I unlocked the doors and we got into the truck.

"Morning's best for this kind of thing," said Chase. He'd kept the passenger door open so that the dim little dome light in the cab stayed on. He drew out a compact commando knife. It looked sharp—and well-used. He began to clean his thumbnail with the point.

"Will there be, like, guards and stuff?"

"Depends."

"So, you're just never going to tell me what we're up to," I said.

"Why don't you settle down." He spat. The husks fluttered to the floor.

"Don't tell me to calm down," I said.

"I said 'settle down'," he replied blandly.

"Whatever. I have a right to know what I've gotten myself into."

"Well, we're not dropping by to pick up a few cans of soup," said Chase looking up from his thumbnail.

"That doesn't mean you have to treat me like an idiot."

"Then quit acting like one."

I opened my mouth to reply with some withering comment, but Chase went on.

"If something goes really wrong and you get arrested and questioned, it's better if you know as little as possible. If anything, it's for your protection."

"Gee, thanks so much for looking out for me."

"I knew I shouldn't've passed on that Camry." He shook his head and spat the shells onto the floor of the cab.

"Do you have to do that? Why don't you spit them out the door? The one that's open?"

He spat some more.

"How long are we going to sit here, then?" I asked, folding my arms. "Can you tell me that, or would it be too dangerous for me?"

He peered up through the windshield into the dark sky. "Let's give it ten minutes and then go."

"Do you have a watch?" I asked.

"No."

"Neither do I."

"So."

"So," I said, "what good is it to say we'll go in ten minutes if we have no way of knowing what time it is? Why not just tell me when you want to go, and we'll go."

"Just be ready," he said.

"I am," I huffed.

He squinted up through the windshield again, as though there were something in the sky only he could read. Then he sheathed the knife.

"Let's go now," he said. "Start her up."

I exhaled my exasperation and turned the key. The engine rumbled up and idled in the cold morning. I switched on the heater. The pink glow of dawn had emerged faintly on the horizon, and now that my eyes were adjusted to the low light, I could make out the countryside around us.

"Which way?" I said.

"Stand by."

Chase fished around in his knapsack and brought out a small, two-way radio. He held it to his mouth and depressed the talk button.

"Mountain Lion's on the move," he said. When he released the button, there was a burst of static and then a tiny electronic beep.

The only response from the other radio was an answering static and the tiny beep.

"Go," said Chase.

"The Mountain Lion, huh?" I laughed.

"It's just 'Mountain Lion'," he said. "No 'the'."

"Right. Mountain Lion," I said laughing. "Grr!"

"Just go."

"Tell me where," I said, putting the truck in gear.

"Head that way." He pointed.

We bounced down through the grass and down the field. I shifted into second, then third. The smaller bumps weren't so noticeable when I drove faster.

"There's a road about a hundred yards past the trees. See? To the left. Get on the road and head east."

"Which way's east?" I asked.

"Toward the sun," he sighed and pointed. "Toward the light."

I steered the Tacoma smoothly through the trees, but the truck's suspension grunted and squeaked in protest as we slammed through the deep trough of a dry ditch. Chase bounced up and bonked his head on the roof of the cab. He braced himself and shot me a look. I slowed as we dipped through the barrow pit and up onto the dirt road, then I turned the truck into the coming dawn.

When Chase finally told me we were raiding a data center, I had envisioned an immaculate, brightly lit building with glass walls and row upon row of computers, the kind with magnetic tape wheels and lots of flashing lights, but instead it was a large, mostly empty office building in middle of a sprawling business park. It lay within the boundaries of a neighboring Zone, but well away from any homes.

I drove with Chase in the growing light until he told me to stop.

"All right," said Chase. "I walk from here. Keep your radio on, but don't transmit unless you absolutely have to. If you don't see us by noon, park the truck at the place, go home, and just lay low."

I knew the plan was for me to wait with the truck, but the prospect of staying there by myself hadn't fully occurred to me until then. I wondered what I would say if an Agency goon found me—if they rolled up in one of their armored vehicles to find me without a chip, nowhere to go, and no way to defend myself. They could arrest me. They could rape me. They could do anything.

"Could I come with?" I asked.

"You want to? Could get dicey."

"I wouldn't want to miss out."

"Well, it'd really be better to stick with the plan. You really want to come along?"

"Yeah. I could probably help." I thought about Arie and me in the neighborhoods. Watching out for each other, splitting up tasks. "Two is better than one."

"Yeah," he said. "I can always use another set of hands."

He passed me a baseball bat.

"Know how to use one of those?"

I swallowed. "I think you hold the skinny end."

"Then let's be on our way."

We walked together further into the business park. There was no one around, but we moved carefully.

"Here," said Chase quietly. We knelt beside a retaining wall.

I recognized the roads and buildings from the map I saw in the gang's ready room at the haunted house.

"Which one is it?" I asked. "That one?"

"No, that one," said Chase, pointing across the street and up the block. It was a dark-colored building with vines creeping up its metal sides.

"You sure?"

"Positive. Why?"

"I dunno," I said. "Looks deserted."

"Yeah, probably just one guy inside. Patrol vehicle drops them off in shifts. Probably just one goon with a sidearm."

Chase produced his pistol. He flicked the cylinder open, then closed. He replaced it in the holster at the small of his back.

"Have you ever shot anyone?" I asked.

Chase looked over, but I couldn't read his face.

"Probably," he said.

"Recently?"

"Nope. And I'd rather not. So, let's be careful."

He reached into his jacket pocket and got out the little radio.

"Hey," I said, pointing to the radio, "can I do it?"

He shrugged and said, "Sure, okay." He smiled and handed it to me.

"What do I say?" I asked.

"Just tell them Mountain Lion is in ready position," he said.

I pressed the soft rubber key and spoke softly into the handset. "The Mountain Lion is in the ready position." Then I turned to Chase.

"Let go of the button," he said.

I winced with embarrassment, and when I did, there came the burst of static and the beeps. A few seconds later came an answering static burst and beeps, and then another.

"It worked?" I asked.

He shrugged again and then nodded.

"What? I did it wrong?"

"It's not 'the' Mountain Lion. It's just Mountain Lion."

"Oh. Right. Sorry."

"And keep the commentary to a minimum," he said with a nod.

"Okay."

"When I get the doors open, tell them we're in."

"Okay."

"We'll cross here," said Chase, "following this line of shrubs. Then to the corner and through that far set of doors. Woolly'll come in from the west. Ruby from the south."

He nodded at the bat. "You said you know how to use that."

"I said I'd do my best, coach."

"Just keep your eye on the ball," said Chase. "Let's go."

We rushed across the street, paused, then moved on. The landscaping around the building was beyond overgrown, and it formed a kind of barrier wall around the building. We stayed low and worked our way up alongside the volunteer trees and enormous tangled hedges to the steel door. We crouched in the shadow of the doorway, and from somewhere inside his coat Chase produced a set of steel picks in a leather slip case. He removed two of them and began poking at the lock.

"Peek in that window," he mumbled, jabbing his chin at the window beside the door.

I peered inside over the bottom edge of the window, the glass of which was filmy from neglect. It was dark inside.

"I can't see anything," I whispered.

"No lights?" he said.

"No. Nothing."

"That's good," said Chase. He opened the door. Then he stood and pocketed the lock tools.

"You're fast," I said quietly.

He shook his head slightly. "Just good." He motioned me in.

As I moved into the unlit space within, I came very close to Chase. It felt like we were nose to nose. Then I stepped inside. Chase flicked on a small flashlight and stuck it in his mouth like a cigar. It shined into the room. I moved farther inside.

"Alison, wait." He took me by the wrist and pulled

me back to him. I turned and faced him again.

His eyes were sharp and shrewd and brown, and when he looked my way I felt as though no detail about me went unnoticed. But there was kindness in his eyes, too.

"What is it?" I whispered. His face was no more than an inch from mine.

"The radio," he said. "Tell them we're in."

"Oh. Right," I breathed. "Sorry."

Without taking my eyes off Chase, I lifted the little radio to my mouth and pressed the key. "The Mountain Lion is inside. I mean—Mountain Lion is inside."

The others answered back by keying their radios, and then we proceeded.

"Seriously, though," I said. "Your signals all have double meanings."

Chase turned and went into the darkness.

I knew there were people in that building, or that there had been recently. For one thing, there were no cobwebs—a dead giveaway. Most buildings and houses abandoned since Year One were draped in thick cobwebs and filled with dust. Most long-vacant buildings had a breach somewhere, like broken windows or doors left open, which allowed astonishing amounts of dirt and dust to accumulate inside. Arie and I had seen houses with so much dirt on the floor that vast indoor gardens of ferns and moss had sprouted.

And then there was the wildlife. Lots of houses had birds inside. We had seen families of raccoons and skunks and squirrels denning up under beds and in closets. We'd seen houses teeming with mice in such numbers that the floors seemed to surge beneath our feet, and there was a windowless supermarket so infested with bats that we'd had to flee from the place before suffocating in its guano stench.

But I didn't have to go inside to know the data center was occupied and cared for. I knew as soon as the door opened. Chronically disused buildings have a certain odor, too, even those that are still weather-tight. A smell of dirt and mildew, but something deeper and richer, too—a loamy smell, the smell of a place made by human hands but ready to be devoured by nature.

The building we'd broken into was not immaculate, but it had at least been swept occasionally, and there was a heat source, too. I wouldn't call it cozy, but it was at least ten degrees warmer than it was outside.

There was an entryway that opened onto a small receiving room, where a corridor stretched to our right and left into the darkness. Chase tapped me on the shoulder and pulled me close so that his mouth was at my ear.

"No sounds," he breathed, still almost too softly for me to hear. "Follow me."

We went to the left, hugging the wall and walking noiselessly. Chase led the way and I followed closely enough to touch his back. It got darker as we got further inside and away from the windows. Chase held his gun in one hand and in the other he had the flashlight—ready to switch on in front of him. From time to time he stopped for as much as a minute to listen.

We followed the corridor and then another, stopping, listening, and then moving on. We'd reached an interior corridor, where there were no windows and nearly no light. At times I wasn't sure if I could see Chase in front of me or if I was only imagining it.

He holstered his gun and then clicked on his flashlight. "Radio," he whispered. I handed it to him. He turned down the volume, and held it close to his mouth.

"Say status," he said.

A few seconds later I heard Woolly's voice faintly in the speaker. "This is Panda. We got nothin'."

Then Ruby: "Godmother. Same."

"All right," said Chase into the radio. "Everyone duck down for a sec. I'm gonna bird dog."

When two bursts of static came over the radio, we retraced our steps to the intersection of four corridors. There was a small waiting area, with two frowzy wingback chairs. Chase told me to huddle behind one of them.

"Stay right there," he said.

Next he motioned for the baseball bat. I handed it to him, and he took a few steps up the corridor until he was lost from my view. My breath grew shallow and the seconds seemed to stretch into hours.

I heard a sharp clack. It resounded loudly but flatly through the corridors. The suddenness of the noise in that stillness made me think a lightning bolt had struck my eardrum, but I knew in fact it was not even as loud as a gunshot. As I heard the soft shuffle of Chase returning, I realized that he had struck the tile floor with the bat.

Chase crouched behind the other chair and we waited, ears straining to detect any noise apart from that of our own breathing.

And then there came a sound.

A door unlatched.

There came the faint squeak of a door hinge, and we saw the glow of an electric light source at the far end of the hallway. We peered around the sides of the chairs.

A man appeared. He stepped out of a room somewhere at the far end of the long hallway, and there he stood, looking our way and holding open the door—

perhaps for the aid of the light emitting from inside the room, or perhaps because the door might lock behind him. He was much too far away to see us in the dimness behind our chairs, but then he switched on a flashlight and shined it in our direction. I scarcely had time to dodge the beam as it swept over the chair, and I thought for sure I'd been spotted.

But all at once the flashlight winked off, and I poked my head up to see. He'd gone back into the room and the door was closing behind him. Then it was dark again.

"I flushed him," said Chase into his radio. "Stand by."

Ruby and Woolly acknowledged.

"All right," whispered Chase. "All we gotta do is get him to come out again without phoning in. He wasn't acting too worried, was he?"

"He didn't seem worried at all," I said.

"Yeah. Okay. Here. Take the bat."

I took it from him.

"Now," he continued, "we're going to go to that door."

"Which one was it?"

"Seventh one on the right. Pay attention. We're going down to that door. Then it's me on the right side, you on the left. Got it?"

"Yeah."

"I'll make a sound. A knock or something. Homeboy comes out. You clobber him."

"Clobber him?"

"With the bat, yeah. We can't kill him. He might be useful. I mean, don't worry—if he's armed and he draws, I'll take care of him."

"No, it's not that."

"What then?"

"I can't just bash someone on the head," I said.

"What do you mean?"

"I mean I can't do that."

"Are you shitting me?"

"He's a person, Chase. A living being."

Chase snorted. He stood up.

"Gimme the bat," he spat. I held it out in the dim light and he snatched it away. He came out from behind the chairs, opened his mouth to say something, but then only scoffed and shook his head. He turned and walked away. I saw his outline for a moment, and then he vanished into the dark hallway.

"Wait!" I hissed. I followed him.

"Thought you had my back," he said. He was whispering, but only just.

"It's not that," I said.

"Ah, just shut up awhile."

He walked fast. No more creeping silently. I tried to keep up, and I knew he'd stopped only when I blundered into him from behind.

Chase's flashlight came on and I saw his face. Tight and annoyed, but calm somehow. He put his flashlight in my hand.

"Shine it on the door," he said. "Like where his face will be when he opens it. Shine it in his eyes."

"You're not going to hit him, are you?"

"Just do it."

I did as he said.

Chase reached out to knock on the door, but then he paused and turned to me.

"A 'living being'?" he asked.

I held the flashlight. Chase knocked on the door.

"What did you think we were gonna do with the bat?" he added. "Play some slow-pitch?"

The man came to the door. He squinted at the flashlight glare. Chase hit him with the bat.

It was quick, efficient. It made me flinch, but it wasn't angry or brutal. The bat came down on the man's head with a wet, meaty sound, and he began to sink to the floor as if a patch of quicksand had materialized beneath him. Chase caught him by the shirtfront and eased him down.

"Don't just stand there," Chase hissed at me. "Help me get him inside."

There was a gash on the man's brow, just at his hairline. It bled steadily, pooling around his eyes and leaving burgundy dots and smears on the floor as we dragged him into the room.

The data center was just that one room. It looked as though it was once a large meeting room, but now it was lined with computers, perhaps fifty of them, set up on long folding tables. And they weren't the kind of computers I'd pictured, beeping and tall with spinning reels of tape. Instead it was as if everyone in the neighborhood had brought in their home computers. The cases were of different sizes and colors and no two alike. Wires and cables snaked between them and in chaotic webs across the floor and it reminded me very much of the cobbled-together systems Arie used. There were monitors and keyboards here and there, and there was a dull soft hum of computer fans. The room was warm with their exhaust.

Chase disarmed the unconscious goon. He'd had a small pistol tucked into his belt. Then Chase checked the room to see if there was anyone else around. It was as he'd said—one goon with a sidearm. We emptied his pockets, then Chase radioed the others and told them where we were. We found a length of stray networking cable and bound the man hand and foot. With much effort we moved him to the center of the room, turned him onto his side, and left him there like some heavy and inconvenient piece of luggage. He lay still awhile, half-awake and muttering.

Chase sat down at a workstation and began scrolling absently through the system. I flopped down in a corner of the room and pouted as Ruby arrived and then Woolly a few minutes later.

Ruby checked on the goon and sorted through his liberated belongings. Then she approached and stood over me.

"What's the matter with you, Kiddo?"

Chase scoffed but didn't look our way.

I didn't answer.

"What happened?" Ruby demanded.

"She got all soft when I told her she had to konk this clown on the head."

"I don't like violence," I said.

"You said you wanted to come," said Chase.

"I didn't know I'd have to do something like that," I said. "I'm the driver, remember?"

"You're not a driver," he shot back. "You're a scared little girl who happens to know how to drive a stick."

"Ease up, Chase," Ruby ordered. "So what if she don't like beating up on people?" She rubbed my back. "Al, you can ignore him. He's a sweet fella, but he's also a real prick."

"She should have stayed with the truck," Chase insisted.

"I didn't want to stay in the truck alone," I shouted. "Okay? I guess that makes me a big chicken."

Woolly came in. "You two again?" he said.

"Stay the hell out of it, Woolly," said Chase.

"Everybody shut the hell up!" Ruby hollered. The room got quiet. "Now. Get to work."

CHAPTER 15

Woolly sat in the room's only chair. It was an old creaky rolling office chair and it seemed ready to buckle under Woolly's prodigious mass as he scooted up to a computer workstation. Chase took a knee beside him. Woolly plugged a small memory stick into a port on the computer case and after a few moments, he began typing furiously.

Ruby was watching over the goon. I sat in my corner and watched Woolly. He typed one command and then another. They appeared as long strings of green letters and symbols, and after each one Woolly hit the Enter key with his pinkie.

But it didn't seem to be going well. On the monitor, there was a procession of error messages and failure notifications. The computer beeped as if annoyed or disappointed.

Woolly let out a soft curse and typed some more.

"We got the goon," said Chase, tilting his head in that direction. "Let's wake him up. Get his credentials."

"Nah. Don't trust him. He might give us some contingency command or fake account that sends out an alert. Let me see if I can get in without him," said Woolly. "Then maybe we'll talk to him."

He typed some more and the computer emitted a

series of beeps that I was sure did not indicate anything good. Woolly cursed again and shook his head.

This went on for what seemed like an hour. Chase kibitzed at Woolly, pointing at the screen and making suggestions. Woolly shook his head sternly. They bickered back and forth.

Woolly said, "I keep telling you—that might work for a sys admin, but this is basically a guest account. Gotta be careful or I'm gonna hit a tripwire and red flags are gonna start going up all over the Agency network. Is that what you want?"

Chase had no reply.

"I didn't think so."

"Okay," said Chase, "but I doubt they're going to be checking often enough to—"

"Chase." Woolly interrupted him, voice raised. "Shush. Gimme a minute."

Chase threw up his hands and was quiet.

"Give me a minute," Woolly reiterated, "to myself. Go away. Let me think." He made a shooing motion.

Chase got to his feet and walked away in a huff. He stood a short distance off, but kept an eye on Woolly's computer monitor. I kept watching.

Woolly's fingers burst into motion and pages of text appeared on the monitor, as if Woolly were consulting some manual or operator notes. He scrolled through numerous pages of text, nodding at times, rubbing his whiskers. Chase began to pace.

"You got this, Wool," said Chase.

Woolly dismissed him with a wave of his beefy hand. He typed something and the text on the monitor vanished.

Then Woolly bowed his head. I thought he might be saying a prayer. But then, with his eyes still closed and head down, he began to type. Slowly and without looking at the monitor, he entered a short command on the keyboard and tapped the Enter key with his pinkie. He entered another command, and another. There were no cross-sounding beeps or long error messages.

Woolly kept his head down a moment longer. Then he opened his eyes and raised his head to see the monitor. Chase stopped pacing and stood looking, arms on his hips. I leaned forward to see better, as if I'd understand anything on the monitor.

Woolly nodded once at the text he saw displayed on the monitor.

Chase and I traded a look. Chase nodded at me and bit his thumbnail.

Next Woolly entered a long series of words and symbols—a command that went on and on. He entered lots of characters, backspaced over some of them, entered more, paused, then typed more. Soon there was a single command that wrapped around almost two complete lines of text. Woolly squinted slightly and traced a fingertip over the green characters, checking, double-checking.

When he seemed satisfied, he placed his index finger over the Enter key. He let it hover there a moment, and then he pressed it.

Nothing happened for several seconds. A blank line appeared beneath Woolly's extra-long command, but nothing else. Then, unceremoniously, there was a single, friendly beep, and a new prompt appeared. I wouldn't have known what to make of it, but Chase clapped and said, "Yes!"

"Okay," said Woolly. "I am—as they say—in."

Chase came up behind Woolly, clapped him on the back, and took a knee by his side again. I got up from the corner and came up behind Woolly. I wrapped my arms around his shoulders, gave him a squeeze, and kissed his whiskered cheek.

"I don't know what just happened," I said, "But, it was magnificent. Well done."

"Thanks, Al," he said, patting my arm. "What's got you in such a good mood all a sudden?"

"After this we look for Arie," I said. "Right?"

"Yep. Looking forward to it."

"I'd give anything to see him again."

"Sounds like a sharp kid," said Woolly.

"Oh, he is smart," I said. "Scary-smart. Like you, Wool. You two will get along great."

It was the first time I'd allowed myself to speak of Arie as though he might still be alive. It was emotionally reckless, I knew, but the situation seemed to call for positive thinking. If Ruby's band of misfits were anything at all, they were positive, and it was infectious.

When Gary told me that Arie was dead, I didn't believe it. Eventually I thought it was simply a matter of denial, of not wanting to believe, of not accepting reality. However, when Ruby hinted that Arie might not be dead after all, a question arose in my mind and gnawed at me: wouldn't I know if he was really gone? Wouldn't a mother know?

Woolly resumed typing his cryptic computer commands. His big hands moved with remarkable deftness over the keys. System beeps emitted from the computer and the contents of files and directories flashed on the monitor.

"We're in business," he said to Chase, still typing. "I'm gonna download as much as I can find, then we'll be ready to talk to this goon you got tied up. This connection is slow as hell, though, and this computer is no Deep Blue. Tell Ruby I'll be ready to roll in—three hours, maybe."

"Ya got two!" Ruby cried shrilly from the other side of the room.

Woolly chuckled. "Tell her one," he said.

I gave him a pat on the shoulder and turned to join Ruby. She was poking the goon with her toe. He moaned a little and stirred as I approached.

"Al, let's get this dope woke up and then pump him for everything he knows."

"Will I have to clobber him at all?"

"Only if you want to." She chuckled.

"Okay," I said.

The goon was awake, still lying on his side with his face caked with drying blood. He turned his head awkwardly to see us. Ruby and I dragged him into a corner and propped him into a sitting position. I sat cross-legged on the floor with him. He was pudgy, unkempt, and shockingly pale, with a reddish-blond beard of sparse curly whiskers. His gloomy blue eyes darted from me to Ruby and the others.

Ruby gathered the contents of the man's pockets into a pile at his feet, and now she sorted through it, inspecting each item before setting it on the floor again. There was a pocket knife, a few ration cards, some keys, papers folded into fourths, and a beat-up stainless-steel pocket flask.

"What's your name?" asked Ruby.

She unfolded the papers and peered at them. It was a series of tables and what looked like computer commands.

"Phil," said the goon. "Phillip. Phillip Carlton. Most people call me P.J."

"Got a family, P.J.?"

"Uh huh."

"How ya feeling'?"

"Head hurts."

"Ya. Sorry about that. Nothing personal. And don't worry. We ain't gonna hurt ya no more."

She picked up the flask and shook it. A liquid sloshed inside.

"Maybe this'll help," she said. "What's in it? Sasparilla?"

"Special brew," said P.J. with a guilty smile.

She twisted off the cap and took a sniff, but then she scrunched her face.

"Brake fluid?"

P.J. nodded. "And other things. Try it. It ain't bad. I water it down, filter it through bread and raisins. Tastes all right."

"P.J., it don't matter if it tastes like cherry cola. This stuff's got ethylene glycol in it. It'll kill ya."

She emptied the flask on the carpeting and then dropped it back in the pile. P.J. watched glumly as it clunked on the floor.

"I don't want you drinkin' that anymore," said Ruby. She felt around in the folds of her coat and presented a flask of her own. "Here. Try a slug a'that." She twisted the cap off and held it to his lips and he drank.

"Smooth," he said.

"Course it is. It's scotch. Have another."

He drank, deeper this time.

"Who are you people, anyway?" said P.J. licking his lips. "Don't you know how much trouble you're in?"

"We'll get to that," said Ruby. "What's this mean?" she showed him the unfolded papers.

"Just my maintenance schedule. And I was already behind when you jerks showed up. Hard enough to keep these junkers running without some chip-rippers whacking me in the face with a—what was that? A baseball bat?"

From someplace else within her coat Ruby found a large folding Buck knife. She flicked it open with a practiced gesture. The blade was as long as my hand and looked very sharp.

P.J. recoiled.

"Ah, don't be a 'fraidy cat," she said. "If I was gonna stick ya, I'd'a done it while you was knocked out. Gimme your hands."

He held out his hands warily and Ruby passed the blade through the strands of network cable. P.J. shook his hands free and then sat rubbing the red grooves in the skin of his wrists. Ruby took a slug from the flask.

"Here," said Ruby, offering it to him. He took it and drank, then gave it back.

"Tell me about alla this, P.J.," said Ruby, gesturing with the point of her knife at the rows of computers.

"What about it?" he said with a shrug. "It's a data center. Databases, account information, you know, for the Agency. We manage data for eight Zones from right here. Me and three other guys in twelve-hour shifts. Personal records, tracking data, ration schedules, security stuff. It's all here on these shitty computers."

"Ya. We done broke into your computers, P.J." She jabbed her thumb at Woolly. "That big fella over there—he done hacked you. 'Zat how ya say it? 'Hacked'?"

P.J. nodded.

"Ya. Well, we're downloadin' what we come for, so you're off the hook for that. But, listen."

P.J. blinked nervously.

She tilted her head in my direction and said, "My friend here used to have a family. A son. Her and him—

that was her whole family. But then they took him away. Your bosses. Now she needs to get some information off'a these computers to find out what they did with him. I want you to help her. Can you do that for me?"

"What if I don't?"

Ruby rolled forward onto her knees and pinned P.J. into the corner. She held the knife to his throat. Her face was close to his.

"Then I'll kill ya," said Ruby. "And then I'll go find any family ya got and kill them, too."

P.J. held still, eyes wide.

Ruby held him there for a few long moments. Then she chuckled and said, "Relax." She eased back onto her haunches. "I already toldja I wasn't gonna hurt ya." She folded the Buck knife and put it away. "But ya get the point, right? We all want to protect those we love, ya know?"

P.J. sighed and nodded sadly.

"We're the good guys, P.J., honest. Them assholes you work for—they're the bad guys. You know it's true. I bet you've seen things. How they do. The hurt they cause. Haven'cha?"

He looked at the floor.

"If ya say you won't help," said Ruby, "we won't hurt ya. But if you do help us, we won't tell no one. You got that konk on your head. You can tell your boss we knocked you out and we was gone when you come to. I can even knock ya back out if you think that'd be better."

"Thanks," said P.J., running a palm over his pallid face. His eyes had begun to glisten with the alcohol.

Ruby held up her flask and P.J. nodded.

He took it from her and drained it.

"Chase," said Ruby.

"Yeah, Boss?" said Chase over his shoulder.

"Come say hi to my new friend, P.J."

Chase rose and joined us in the corner. He shook P.J.'s hand.

"Who do you report to, P.J.?"

"His name is Chandler."

"We know him," said Ruby, trading a nod with Chase. "He's a class-A prick. A real role model for pricks everywhere."

P.J. shrugged his agreement.

Chase spoke to P.J. of Zone boundaries and security and chains of command. P.J. named Agency managers and supervisors. Ruby took notes on the back of P.J.'s maintenance schedule, scribbling with the nub of a pencil, but Chase and Ruby already knew much of what P.J. revealed.

I knew two or three Agency goons by name—Gary Gosford among them. Few Agency goons ever actually introduced themselves, and aside from a couple medical techs, I'd never even spoken to an actual officer of the Agency. Ruby seemed to know almost more than P.J.

After a half hour or so, Chase said he'd heard enough. He shook P.J.'s hand again and rejoined Woolly. Ruby stood stiffly and stretched her chubby legs.

"Nice talkin' with ya, P.J.," she said. She put out her hand and he shook it. She pocketed the papers but returned his other things. "Just sit tight."

He nodded sleepily.

Ruby chucked me on the arm. "Keep him company, will ya? Tell him about your boy."

"Okay."

Ruby turned away and directed a procession of profane encouragement toward Woolly, presumably to make him work faster. Woolly stuck to his original time estimate of one hour, explaining in his placid and articulate way that he was unable to alter the way computers worked. I turned back to P.J.

"Was it you that hit me on the head?" he said, gingerly fingering the laceration. It had stopped bleeding, but it had swelled and turned purple. It looked painful.

"No," I said. "I was holding the flashlight."

P.J. nodded.

"So," I said, searching for something to say, "how long you been a goon?"

He sighed. "I'm not a goon. And it's not like I volunteered. When I came to, they told me what to do. I've been coming here since then. People from gen-pop call me a goon. To me, it's my job. I have a family, too. A wife and a couple of sons."

"My son got sick and the Agency took him away and wouldn't tell me what happened. I haven't seen him since."

He swallowed. "Sorry."

"It's not your fault."

We sat there awhile.

"When was that?" he said.

"What? My son? Last month."

"I could look him up for you," he said.

"Could you?"

P.J. wetted his lips and looked around the room. Then he nodded. I pulled him to his feet and steadied him as he hopped to one of the workstations and knelt at the keyboard. Woolly rolled the office chair over and we set P.J. on the seat.

Ruby saw us and hustled over. "What's going on? He helpin' with the Arie situation?"

"He said he can look him up. Maybe we can find out what happened."

Ruby beamed. "P.J., I knew you was all right. But no

143

tricks."

A wan smile showed on P.J.'s pale face as he typed. Chase came to my side. Woolly watched intently.

We stood there watching the monitor as P.J. entered a username and password. He pressed the Enter key, but nothing happened, and nothing kept happening for a minute or two.

"If this is a trick," said Woolly, "we're going to have a problem."

"Is it not working?" I asked.

"P.J.," said Ruby. "This better not be a trick."

"No, it's not that," said P.J. "I'm logging into one of the central databases. It's off-site. Our connections are really slow."

"We've noticed," said Woolly.

At last a new prompt appeared on the monitor, and we all leaned in to see.

"Okay," said P.J. "How do you spell his name?"

I told him. He typed it.

There was another series of commands. P.J. typed almost as fast as Woolly. He hit the Enter key with an emphatic flourish.

"Okay. It's searching. I don't have privileges to access his full record, but I'm pretty sure it will show me his profile code. That'll at least tell us where he's at. If he's anywhere, I mean. Sorry it's so slow."

"Woolly," said Ruby, "you know about this profile thing?"

Woolly shook his head and nodded at the same time. "A little. It's encoded into the chips," he said, tapping his neck. "Right?"

"Yeah," said P.J. "Everyone's got a profile," said P.J., turning in his seat and looking up at us. "It's basically the Agency's shorthand for a person. A summary. First four numbers are the Zone you're assigned to. Next is your illness status—whether or not you take the serum, your dosage, annual treatment date. Next is employment status, rations, living arrangements, things like that. There's some other codes I'm not sure about. The last few numbers indicate your age."

Woolly raised his eyebrows and nodded approvingly.

"Wool, you want some paper to write all this down?" I asked.

"Nah," said Woolly. Then he tapped his temple and grinned. "I got it."

After P.J. typed more commands and we'd waited several minutes, Arie's full name appeared, followed by the long string of numbers P.J. mentioned. Seeing his name that way—glowing green search results on a computer monitor—it almost made Arie alive again. My breath hitched, and I was suddenly as sure as I'd ever been that he must be alive.

"Okay," said P.J. "This says he's in Zone 1891. Where was he when he was taken?"

"In that Zone," said Chase.

"Oh," said P.J. "Okay, well, that's no help, then. I wonder if he had a location account."

"What's that?" asked Woolly.

"You know we can track you using your ID chip, right?"

We all nodded.

"Right, well, it's a passive system. It's not real-time or anything. The battery's tiny and we couldn't handle real-time tracking telemetry for every single person, anyway. So, most people never get tracked at all. Only people who are interesting in some way—usually people who are up to something."

"So?" said Woolly.

"So, if one of the officers wants to track a user, we have to open a location account. Let's see if Arie's got one," said P.J. He typed a few commands. "Yeah. He's been tracked."

"Show us," said Woolly.

"Okay," he said. "But only because I'm a little drunk. I could get in a shit-load of trouble for this."

"We really appreciate it," I said.

P.J. produced a spreadsheet on the monitor. Line after line of information, mostly numerical.

"Here you go. GPS coordinates, times. Looks like my bosses were really interested in your son."

"Where are all these places?"

"No way to say for sure without a GPS system and a basemap, but I'm assuming this location is your house." He pointed to a number on the monitor that appeared most often. "This one is probably the depot where you get supplies. Look at these, though. I'm not cartographer, but these have got to be way outside your Zone. This Arie guy really got around."

I chewed my lip.

"I assume alla you guys are chip rippers?" asked P.J.

"That's confidential," said Ruby.

I wanted to ask him if I'd been tracked. Or rather, how much I'd been tracked. Gary told me he knew that my chip went dead. What else did he know about Arie and me?

"We've got to wrap this up," said Chase, tapping his wrist. "It's just about quitting time for P.J. here. His replacement will arrive in about an hour."

"Oh, yeah," said P.J. "Hey, I know you're busy, but will you guys tie me up again before you take off?"

"Course we will, Peej," said Ruby. "We're all friends now."

"Thanks."

Woolly held up his memory stick. "I've got what I came for. I'm taking off." He headed for the door.

"Al," said Chase, "we oughta be going, too."

"What else can you tell me about Arie?" I asked P.J. "Where is he now?"

P.J. toggled back to the previous display. "Let's see. Says he's taking the serum and his treatment date is January second. Sound right?"

"Yeah," I said.

"All right. Ration code is 105; subsistence level. That's no help, either. Housing code—family of two, single dwelling?"

"Yes," I said.

"Okay. Well, all that's left is his age—oh." His hand went to his mouth. "Oh, shit."

"What?" I said. I bent forward to see. "Three zeros? What's that mean?"

P.J. turned to me with a bleak expression. He shook his head. "I'm sorry."

But wouldn't I know? Wouldn't a mother know?

"Sorry, Al," said Chase. He stepped away.

Ruby placed her hand on my neck. She pulled me into the folds of her coat, and I cried.

CHAPTER 16

My knuckles were white from gripping the steering wheel as we drove away from the data center.

"Al? You okay?" asked Chase.

"Of course, I'm not okay," I said.

Chase was quiet for a few minutes. Maybe he had nothing to say. Maybe he was trying to think of something. I didn't care. All I could think about was the Agency and what they had done to Arie.

"I want you to find me a gun," I said finally.

"What? Why?"

"What's the difference? That's what you do, right? Get things? Well, get me a gun."

I pushed down on the gas pedal. The truck bounced across the rough surface of the hay fields.

"You said you don't like violence. Guns are very violent, Alison. Do you even know how to shoot one?"

"I'll figure it out."

I stared straight ahead but without really seeing. I was on auto-pilot, but with an objective: justice for Arie.

"Listen," said Chase, "I know you're angry—"

"Angry? Angry doesn't begin to describe it. They were following him. Why? What reason could they possibly have? And then he mysteriously gets sick? Goes missing? Then he dies? They can't do this. I'll take them out one by one if I have to."

I was starting to realize that, on the one hand, Arie's death was senseless, but in a way some parts of it actually made sense. All the attention Gary paid to us—was he involved? Did Arie discover something dangerous? Is that why he had an encoded journal?

"This is the grief talking, Al, not you. It's totally understandable. Getting your hopes up, then finding out he really is gone—"

I pounded on the steering wheel. "He's not gone! Arie is not dead! I know he's not! They've taken him. They've taken my son."

"Just tell me what you're planning on doing with a gun."

I started to cry. "I don't know. I just—I have to do something."

Chase put his hand on my shoulder, and I was mildly surprised that the tenderness in his touch actually had a sedating effect. My shoulders relaxed and my fingers loosened around the wheel.

"Alison," he said, "I don't know you very well, but I do know that you're not a killer. We can figure this out. I'll help you. But don't let your anger make you blind. You'll make a mistake and it'll all be over for you, and then you'll be in no position to help anyone."

I breathed in ragged gulps of air to avoid crying uncontrollably.

"If your kid really is out there somewhere, he needs you to keep it together right now—not lose it."

What he said was right, but my jaw clenched. What was I supposed to do with this rage? With this sense of complete helplessness?

"I wouldn't be a good mother if I didn't fight for my son." I looked over at Chase. "Just get me a gun."

*

Chase tromped along in front of me without speaking as we wound through the shadowy bowels of the haunted house. Ruby and Woolly had gotten back already and sat on benches at the table eating. I smelled the sour but homey scent of stewed cabbage.

Glen stood at a high table where he stirred a pot with a wooden spoon. "Come eat up," he said.

Chase grabbed a bowl and Glen dished up some cabbage for him. Chase took a seat on the bench across from Woolly and tore a hunk from a loaf of dark, coarse bread.

I wasn't hungry. Glen offered me a bowl and I shook my head.

"How about a game?" Woolly asked Chase.

Chase nodded, but his expression was dark.

Woolly jammed his hand into the cargo pocket of his shorts and produced a miniature folding chess board with tiny magnetic chessmen.

They set up the board and Chase made an opening move. The two men noisily slurped up spoonfuls of the cabbage. I realized that many of the utensils there had been lifted from the fake scenes of terror in the haunted house. A beverage tankard shaped like a human skull, beakers and bowls from the mad scientist's lab. When I came to the table, Woolly scooted over on the bench to make space.

"Are you doing okay?" Woolly asked me.

I hunched my shoulders and nodded.

Ruby plopped a bowl in front of me and it splashed onto the table.

"Eat," she said. "You're going to need your strength."

I took a bite of cabbage. It was mostly flavorless and tepid, but it was comforting.

Gracie walked up to me holding a piece of paper and a broken crayon.

"I drew this for you," she said. "So that you can remember."

She handed me a paper with two stick figure drawings. Arie and me. To remember him. Arie would certainly approve. Without cameras, Gracie's likenesses of Arie and I would have to do, and like all crayon portraits rendered by children, this one was not only oddly accurate but deeply affecting. I knew Arie was fond of Gracie. It would be impossible not to be. If only he could have gotten to know her better.

"I love it," I told her. "Thank you."

She smiled at me and I wrapped my arms around her. She squeezed me around the middle. Then I saw that she had lost a tooth.

That's how things are with kids, I thought. They're always changing and progressing. Even when we're not ready for it. They're always moving on—even when we don't want that, when we want them to stop and wait for us to catch up. Gracie sat beside me and rested her head on my arm. We watched Woolly and Chase play their game.

I suddenly thought of how she'd been watching our house and something occurred to me.

"Gracie," I said. "Remember how you used to hide in my backyard? And Arie would bring you food?"

"Yeah."

"Did you ever see anyone else around there? Anyone hiding or following Arie?"

She looked at Ruby.

"S'alright, kiddo. You can tell Al."

151

Gracie swallowed and nodded again.

"Who was it? Agency men?"

She nodded again.

"Do you know who they were? Or what they wanted?"

"No," she said so quietly I almost couldn't hear her. She turned away from me. "I don't want to talk about this anymore." She walked away and lay down on the pallet bed in the corner of the room.

Ruby shook her head. "I think they did something to her. You know? We found her half-starved and scared to death that we'd take her to the Agency." She scowled.

"Check," said Woolly.

Chase frowned and moved his king.

"So, what are we up to, anyway?" I asked. "The stealing, the hacking, the secret plans."

"Guess you oughta know everything"—Ruby tapped her neck to indicate where her chip used to be— "now that you're really one of us."

"Check," said Woolly again.

"Dammit," muttered Chase.

"We don't think it's like this everywhere," said Ruby. "The way we are. We got no memories. We're barely surviving. It can't be like this everywhere, and if it is, it shouldn't be. Know what I'm saying?"

I'd thought about this a lot—before I'd ever met Ruby, I'd wondered. Arie had, too. The Agency told us staying healthy was a matter of containment, quarantine. There was suspicion, of course. I was dubious about everything, almost from the moment I woke up in the infirmary, and so were a lot of people. But there was no TV, no Internet, and few utilities. We could talk to one another, but there was no way to trust anything we heard, no way to know what was going on even fifty miles away, let alone out in the rest of the world. The fences and patrols kept us penned up like sheep, but it was the lack of information that really isolated us.

"Yeah," I answered. "Of course. But how can we know? How can we establish what's really going on? Or what really happened?"

"Those are the questions we're working on," Ruby said, squinting one eye and jabbing her chubby finger at me.

"Something happened," Chase said glumly. "I've seen the graves."

"It's safe to assume there was a global pandemic," Woolly said. "The evidence is there. It's in newspapers and recordings that pre-date Year One. It's the memory effects of the serum, obviously, that are suspect."

"So, what do we do?"

"Figure it out, Al," said Woolly. "Start from the assumption that the pandemic was real, and that the need for the serum is real, but the memory effects are unnecessary."

I thought about it. "Well," I said, "We need to find a way to keep our memories or get them back. Because if we keep losing our memories, we just stay in the dark."

"Correct," said Woolly. "But we also need the serum. And if we're assuming that the supposed memory-erasing effects of the serum are simply a measure to control us, to keep us in the dark, as you say, then it's not the serum we're afraid of, is it? What we have to worry about is—" he trailed off and held up his hand to let me finish the thought.

"What we have to worry about is taking the serum from *them*," I said. "It's not the serum. It's something else. It's a treatment or drug they add in or give us at the same time."

"Check," said Woolly.

Chase bonked the table with his fist. "Dammit!" He moved his king again.

"So," I said, "we steal the serum before they put in the memory-erasing part."

Woolly nodded.

"And we give it to ourselves," I said.

Woolly moved his queen across the board. "Checkmate."

Chase tossed his spoon into his empty bowl, then got up to get more cabbage.

"So, that's why we broke into the computer room?" I asked. "To find out if this is all true?"

"Yes," said Woolly, taking a bite of the dark bread. "Or, more accurately, to find out where the serum is stored so that we can steal it and test our hypothesis."

"But," said Chase.

"But what?" I said.

"My computer bit the dust today," said Woolly. "Power surge or something. Or it overheated. The mo-bo melted like a s'more."

"Toldja you should have lifted a couple from the data center," said Chase.

"Yeah," said Woolly with an exasperated sigh. "You've mentioned that. I can build another one."

"With what? You got no parts. You got no source for parts. You got no source for a source for parts."

"I'm gonna check with that old guy out by the bridge who fixes radios."

Chase laughed. "Nope. I checked. He doesn't know a hard drive from a hole in the ground."

"I've got computers," I said.

"I'll just have to keep looking," said Woolly.

"Better look faster," said Chase, tapping his wrist.

"Tick-tock."

"Hey," I said, my voice raised. "Guys. I've got hard drives."

They looked at me as if they'd forgotten I was there.

"My son collected them. Computers, cables, adapters. Lots of hard drives. Piles of computer parts."

Woolly raised one eyebrow, as if I'd just said something suggestive. "When you say, 'lots of hard drives'—"

"I mean boxes of hard drives," I said. "Some are new, haven't even been used. Dozens, maybe. All kinds of parts."

Chase grimaced. "No wonder I could never find any."

"This is the last piece of a big old puzzle," said Ruby. She leaned forward and squeezed my arm. "Wool's finally got the files. If he can get his computer back up and runnin', we can really make some head-way. Then we can find out what happened to Arie."

"So, this will really work?" I asked. "We'll keep our memories—and not get sick?"

Ruby grinned. "That's the idea."

"And what if they catch us?" I asked.

Chase was scrutinizing the little chessboard and his humiliated king. "Checkmate," he said.

"Yeah," said Woolly. "So, let's not let it get to that point. Let's go computer shopping. Alison, you driving?"

"Wait till dusk," said Ruby holding up a cautionary finger. "Don't attract any attention."

"There's just one thing," I said.

"What is it?" Ruby asked.

"I want a gun," I said.

Chase frowned at me. "That's not a good idea. Ruby, you know it's not."

155

"What're you wanting a gun for?" Ruby asked.

"I just do."

Chase shook his head slowly. Ruby just chuckled.

"Tell you what," she said. "I'll see what I can do."

*

The truck was a big mistake after all. The people in my Zone were accustomed to seeing Agency patrol vehicles, and maybe the occasional gas-powered scooter, but not loud, fully functioning pickup trucks. Automobiles were not illegal, but they were quite rare. From behind their curtains and blinds, my neighbors peeked out as the Tacoma rumbled conspicuously through the streets, weaving past the debris and the hulks of abandoned cars. Woolly stood in the truck bed bracing himself on the roll bar.

By the time we reached my street, people were stepping out onto their porches to watch. Woolly waved at them like some humongous pageant queen on a parade float.

"Gosh, this is how rumors start," I moaned, slouching in the seat as low as I could.

"You didn't tell me you lived in the burbs," said Chase, waving at a little boy who ran alongside us. "Don't these rubes not have anything better to do?"

"We're driving through their yards," I said.

"They're gonna think we're newly married."

"Don't flatter yourself."

Chase laughed. "Methinks the lady doth protest too much."

I parked in the driveway of my house. It was the first time I'd seen a car of any kind there.

Woolly began to climb down out of the bed. At least twenty people gathered on the perimeter of my yard.

"Let's go, let's go," Chase said, heading to the front

door. "We're attracting attention." He waved at the people. They waved back.

"You think?" I said. I prayed Gary wasn't inside waiting for me. I went to the door and unlocked it.

"Anyone here?" I called as I opened the door.

"Who are you talking to?" Chase asked.

"No one," I said.

"Then why'd you ask if anyone was here?"

"I don't know," I said. "Habit?"

He narrowed his eyes.

Woolly clapped his big meaty hands and then rubbed them together. "Al? Where's the stuff?"

"In the den past the kitchen. I'll show you."

"No need," he said, and with that he pulled a flashlight from the pocket of his denim shorts and clicked it on. Then he scooched his bulky frame around us and continued into the dark of the den. Chase gave me a questioning look but then followed after Woolly.

Just a few seconds later, the beam of Woolly's flashlight came wobbling back into the living room, followed by Woolly himself carrying a huge plastic tote of Arie's computer parts.

"I'll be back," he said as he passed by.

Chase was close behind with a second load. He nodded his head and went out, and soon they came back for more. I stood there in the living room and thought about Arie's collection and how long it had taken to assemble. I wondered to myself what he'd think about Chase and Ruby and Woolly. I was at least happy the computers and adapters and other electronics would not sit in this empty house and be covered over with dust— it was good to know they might help us out after all.

When Chase and Woolly had made several trips apiece, Woolly came into the house and stood in front of me. He had a contented smile on his face and he bowed at the waist.

"Once again," he said, "you have bailed us out of a very tight situation, Al. My thanks to you and your son. Shall we?" He gestured at the door as if inviting me to dance.

The evening air was cool—fresh and alive. As I started up the Toyota, I felt fresh, too. And alive. Maybe it was again that inextinguishable optimism of Ruby and her little team. Maybe it was having friends in the house where Arie and I had lived. It definitely had to do with the prospect of not losing our memories anymore—the thought of that was like the thought of salvation. Only the hope of seeing Arie again was brighter to me, and as we drove out of my neighborhood under the strange and fascinated gazes of my neighbors, I was sure that with Ruby's help, I was going to find out what happened to my son.

Even if I had to kill to find out.

Even if it killed me.

CHAPTER 17

Woolly went to work with the computer cases and parts the moment we got back. He unfastened the screws on the back of one of Arie's old computers and began pulling out circuit boards and cables as if he were cleaning the innards of some animal. Then he cracked open another of the cases. He examined each component before sorting it, nodding or shaking his head as to their usefulness.

We stood around him for a while, watching, thinking maybe it would take him only a few minutes or an hour. Soon he looked up at us.

"What?" he said. "What are you waiting for? Leave me alone. This is gonna take me some time."

We wandered off. I sat down on the worn-out old sofa in the far corner of the room. The armrests were frowzy, and on the cushions were overlapping stains in disturbing shades. I idly thumbed a book I found nearby. Chase sat at the table and opened a wooden chess set, arranging the pieces into various positions. As I watched him, I began to nod off to the sound of beeps and the whir of computer fans and Woolly's grunted curses.

Sometime early in the morning I awoke to a shout of success. I opened my eyes just as Woolly spun around in his computer chair with a wide grin on his face.

"I've got a location. Wake up, kids. It's time to plan." His face was puffy with the lack of a night's sleep, but his eyes twinkled. He winked at me and then spun around to face his monitor.

Chase's face was tucked into the crook of his elbow on the table where he'd likewise fallen asleep. His face was crisscrossed with lines left from the wrinkles in his shirt sleeve. He smiled weakly and nodded his approval.

Ruby stirred from a chair she had settled into. She struggled to stand and limped over to Woolly.

"How far?" Chase asked, his voice froggy with fatigue.

"Two hours. Give or take," Woolly said. "A chemical refinery, great big compound up in North Richmond. We're looking for warehouse 8234-C."

"Think it'll be guarded?" Ruby asked.

"Definitely," said Chase.

Gracie had woken up, too. She climbed onto Woolly's lap, sleepily wrapping her arms around his giant neck and burying her face in his chest. He shifted her gently so that he could reach the keyboard.

"It's a pretty big site," he said, zooming and panning over an aerial map displayed on his monitor.

Yawning and stretching, we gathered around him to see better.

"Several buildings," he said, pointing. "Entrance here. Checkpoint here. That's where the guards'll be. Warehouse is over"—he scrolled the map to one side—"here."

I looked at Ruby. She clasped her hands together and rubbed them vigorously.

"Today's the day, kids," she said. "Today is the day."

Woolly nodded and patted Gracie's back.

Ruby sharply clapped her hands, once, and then

started barking orders.

"Somebody get Glen and that little fart Carlos over here. Chase, you find them maps we swiped a while back."

Gracie scampered over to Ruby and said, "What can I do?"

"Gosh, I dunno, Gracie. Oh, I know—see if you can find us something to eat."

I waited for her to give me something to do, but she seemed to have forgotten me. But then I caught her eye.

She grinned at me with a sort of larcenous squint, then said, "Ah and you. I got something special for you. Come on over here, Al."

She motioned me over to a battered ammo box. From inside it she produced a bundle of oily cloth. She unwrapped it to reveal a small revolver.

"Got you a gun," she said. "Here. Hold out your hand."

I did and she gave me a box with a handful of bullets inside.

"Let's go outside," she said, "and I'll teach you to use it."

The winter sun was just rising and the air was brisk. Ruby seemed to have a kind of pride or satisfaction in having gotten me the gun.

"Now, we can't practice as much as we need to on account of not having many bullets and we don't wanna attract all kindsa attention, but let's take a few shots."

She pressed a button or tab with her thumb and the cylinder fell open. I held out the small box and she removed six bullets.

"See here?" said Ruby. "These holes? They go in like that."

One by one she dropped the bullets into the cylinder.

I watched carefully, but her hands moved so quickly.

"Then ya slap it shut."

She tilted the pistol with a smooth motion and the cylinder fell into place with a neat *click*.

Before she handed it to me, she said, "First rule is you never point it at no one unless you're ready to kill."

*

Later that day, when everyone had arrived, we circled around the computer.

"We'll come in right here," said Ruby, pointing at Woolly's monitor. "Woolly says the serum's in here. We don't know where at exactly, but we'll figure that out. Grab as much as you can, along with anything else that looks useful. But don't hang around too long. We gotta haul ass on outta there."

"Goons? Guards? How many?" asked Carlos.

"There's bound to be some security," said Chase. "But it's such a remote facility we're counting on just a few goons—no Agency troops or vehicles."

It was already getting dark as Ruby outlined the rest of the plan. Once again, we'd ride out before dawn. I was the only one who could drive a stick and Chase was best with a gun, so he would ride with me in the truck. The rest—Glen, Carlos, Ruby, and Woolly—would ride in the only other vehicle they had, a beat-up old Ford Taurus that used to be a police car. The decals and markings had been removed, but you could see the outline of stripes and lettering on the hood and fenders if you looked at it from the right angle. The holes on the roof where the lights had been were filled in with putty. The old Taurus still had its spotlight though, and Ruby said the car had "great get-up-and-go."

"All right," said Ruby. "That's the plan." Then she added, "Any questions?" but she didn't wait for us to ask any. "Good. Let's get a few hours of shut-eye and then head on out."

CHAPTER 18

We stretched and yawned in the darkness, but there was the crackle of anticipation in the dry, chilly air. I stood in the doorway at the back of the haunted house as I watched the others double-check their equipment and murmur last-minute contingencies. Chase and Carlos divvied up their meager stockpile of ammunition. Woolly had a collection of pry-bars, bolt cutters, and sledgehammers in a large canvas tool bag. It clanked heavily as he heaved it into the trunk of the Taurus. At the front of the car, Ruby and Glen had the hood propped up and were checking the clamps on a makeshift hose repair Glen had made.

"Where are the keys?" said Ruby.

Glen held them up and jangled them. "I'll drive," he said as he slammed the hood closed.

"My ass," said Ruby. "Gimme them."

As we made ready to leave, I said, "Hey. What about Gracie?"

"What about her?" Ruby asked.

"Who'll watch her while we're gone?"

"Oh, she'll be fine," said Ruby.

I laughed incredulously. "You've got this place wired with explosives. You can't just leave her here."

Gracie had been sitting forlornly in the dark

anteroom of the haunted house as we got ready to go. She was petting a toy stuffed lamb as though it were a cat or puppy. There was water and food in the haunted house, enough to last for several weeks, probably. And there were beds. Gracie seemed consigned to stay there by herself, but she looked up when she heard us talking about her.

"I can come?" she asked, her back straight.

"Hell no, you can't come," Ruby barked. "Al, if you think we're going to bring her with us, you've lost your mind. This is gonna be dangerous."

"I don't think we should bring her along," I said. "I'm just saying we can't leave her here alone."

"She's taken care of herself almost this whole year," said Carlos. "She ain't no regular kid."

"But she is a kid," I said. Maybe it was the way Arie had taken care of her that made me feel responsible. Or maybe it was motherly instincts. "Don't we have anyone else that can watch her?"

"Lemme come with you!" Gracie said. "I'll be quiet. And won't get in the way. I promise."

"Ain't enough room in the car, kid," Glen snapped. "Not with Woolly and Carlos and alla them guns in back."

"No, I already called shotgun," said Woolly.

"I told you, jeffe," Carlos objected. "You gotta be outside to call shotgun. You can't just call it two days before—"

"Oh, would you two knock it off," snarled Ruby.

"Maybe someone could stay with her," I suggested.

"No way," Ruby said. "We need all the help we can get."

"Then what if she rode with me and Chase until we get close to the compound?" I suggested. "We could drop her off somewhere and pick her up on the way back. She'd only be alone while we're at the warehouse. We're not going to be in there long, right?"

"The place'll be guarded, Al," Ruby said. "There'll be guns."

"But only a couple guards, right? Isn't that what you said, Chase?"

"Well, I think so, but I don't know for sure," Chase answered. "Could be one, could be dozens."

"We could give her a radio," I said. "Leave her with some snacks? I don't know. I just hate the thought of her being alone so long."

Ruby and Chase exchanged glances.

"I really think she'd be fine here," said Ruby. "But if yer gonna keep yapping about it and keepin' us from leavin', then I guess we can bring her along. But you're responsible for her."

"Hear that, Gracie? Let's go!"

Gracie jumped up and clapped her hands together, then ran into my arms.

When we got outside and unlocked the truck, Chase shook his head and said, "You are nothing but trouble."

"I don't think she'll be a problem," I said.

"I wasn't talking about her," he replied.

"Oh," I said, "in that case I agree with you."

Chase regarded Gracie warily as she climbed into the passenger-side jump-seat of the cab. I tightened my ponytail and started the truck.

We drove out of Thrill Harbor and along a back road. We kept our headlights off, driving slowly. Ruby and the others followed us in the Taurus. Chase gave me directions and he relayed them to Ruby using the walkie-talkie.

The drive was tedious, down narrow dirt roads and

over the grown wild farm fields blanketed thinly with the remaining snow. We wound through the quiet, motionless traffic jams of the paved highways. Some of the time we drove with the running lights on and sometimes with no lights. Gracie lay curled up in the jumpseat and was asleep most of the time.

It took us more than two hours to drive just forty miles. The sky had just begun to turn pink when we closed in on the North Richmond industrial park.

"Okay," said Chase. "In a half mile or so we're gonna hit an intersection. There's a ranch house there. We'll drop off Gracie."

"Gracie?" I said. "Wake up, sweetie."

Chase keyed his walkie-talkie and said, "We're stopping."

Gracie looked so pathetic there in the front yard of the dilapidated ranch house. She wore a heavy winter coat and boots, and her hair was wild. My heart broke a little, and I began to doubt my idea of bringing her along instead of leaving her in the relative safety of the haunted house. We left her with a blanket, a jug of water, and a few wild apples.

"Go on in the house, Gracie," I said, trying to sound like everything was fine. "You can watch through the window. We'll be back soon."

Gracie turned to the house but then shook her head. "It's too scary."

I had to chuckle a little at that, considering she'd been living for several weeks in the haunted house of a derelict amusement park.

"It will be light soon," I told her. "Will you go in then?"

"Okay," she said.

Ruby waved goodbye, and she and the others in the

Taurus drove off, planning to circle around and approach the warehouse complex from the far side.

I got back into the truck, but stayed still watching Gracie for a few moments trying to build up the courage to leave her.

Chase rolled his eyes and said, "Jeeze, quit it, wouldja? She'll be fine. She's a tough little runt."

I sighed and started the truck. We drove for a few miles. It was getting light.

"There's a road up here a couple miles," said Chase. "It turns off to the right. You'll see the complex of buildings. There'll be a chain link fence around it."

We came to the road and I turned.

"Okay. This is it. In a couple miles, you'll see the fence. I'm gonna need you to drive through it."

"What do you mean 'drive through it'?"

"I mean drive through the fence."

"Really?"

"Really. You'll need to be going faster, though."

I gave it some gas.

"Faster," said Chase.

"How much faster?"

"Fifty. Sixty."

"We won't crash?"

"That's up to you," he said, without taking his eyes from the road ahead. "When we get through the fence, you'll see a little building kinda off by itself. That's where we're going. Stop right by the door. As soon as we're through the fence, put on the brakes. Not too hard, though."

I looked over at him. He gave me a sly smile. Then he reclined his seat and put one foot up on the glove box.

The speedometer read sixty when I saw the compound. It was some kind of processing facility, like a cannery. There was an old factory and a series of warehouses. It was coming up fast.

"See the gate?" said Chase. "That's where we'll go through." He'd slouched back in the seat with his arm draped over his knee, as if we were on a summer road trip.

"I don't think I—"

"Don't think, Al," he said with a wave of his hand. "Just go on through." He stole a glimpse of the speedometer. "And don't slow down."

I pressed the gas pedal.

Chase put his seat back upright and from under his coat he removed a pistol. Not like Ruby's or mine. It was in better shape, well cared for. He let the cylinder fall open, eyed the chambers, and slapped the cylinder home again. Then he got out his radio.

"This is Mountain Lion," he said. "We're here."

The Tacoma thundered down the road, throwing up bits of asphalt and debris.

"Don't slow down," said Chase. He didn't shout it at me. He didn't seem excited or panicked, nor did he act as if anything particularly unusual was happening.

With my face frozen in a test-pilot grimace and my arms locked out straight, we rammed the gate. There was a heart-shaking crash, the chain link fabric made a high ringing sound with the impact, and we were jolted forward into our seat belts with the deceleration. The side windows of the truck shattered as the fencing wrapped around the truck, sending crumbs of safety glass flying like sea spray. The clattering chain link gate clung to the hood and fenders like some destroyed animal, and there was a deep thudding as the gate posts were wrenched from the ground like great steel carrots.

We rocketed into the compound.

"Brakes," said Chase. "Brakes!"

I stomped the brake and we were pitched forward once more. I felt sure that the truck bed would flip up behind and over top of us. Chase braced himself hard on the dash with one hand and held up his pistol in the other as the truck swerved sideways into a juttering skid.

From somewhere in my mind came the impulse to steer into the skid and so we swerved in that direction, and I somehow avoided over-correcting.

"This building," cried Chase, signaling desperately, but by then we were almost past it. "Stop stop stop!"

I stood on the brake pedal, pulling myself up on the steering wheel so that my butt came out of the seat. The wheels locked up and the tires made a rough howling as we shuddered to a stop.

"Stay right here!" he shouted. "Stay put!"

The passenger door had flown open before we came to rest and Chase was gone from his seat before I managed to look over. I suddenly felt very concerned for him and I craned around inside the truck to see where he'd gone.

It was a small brick building with floor-to-roof windows on all four sides—a dispatch office of some kind—and I'd overshot it by a hundred feet or so. Chase sprinted toward it. He flung open the door and went in, and through the windows I saw a struggle. I thought I heard shouting, and then there was gunfire.

The truck had stalled when we'd skidded to a stop, and it took a few tries to get it started again, but when I did, I u-turned to better see what was happening. Inside the office, two people had taken hold of Chase. They held him by the arms. A third trained an assault rifle on him. Through the glare of the morning sun on the window, I thought I saw Chase look my way.

I'd only known him for a short time, and so far, I wasn't too impressed. He was rude and self-important and reckless. But as I sat in the cab of the Tacoma, with the rubble of broken auto glass in my lap and the steering wheel gripped tight in my bloodless fists, I knew I had to help him. Whether it was because I wanted to find Arie or because I cared for these people, something reflexive and maternal ignited inside me.

I slammed the truck into gear, stomped on the accelerator, and the let the clutch pop out. The rear tires chirped on the pavement and I aimed directly at the building as the little truck surged forward. With a little over a hundred feet before impact, I got it up to only about thirty miles an hour, but that was enough to elicit terrified sideways expressions from everyone inside the building, including Chase.

The two who were holding him jumped out of the way, and Chase did, too, but the other man turned in my direction and pointed the rifle at me. I saw pale orange flashes as he fired at me, but the nose of the Tacoma came blasting through the tall window, and I hit him square-on. The rifle flew away spinning, and the man was tossed like a limp doll through the window on the far side of the small office. He landed on the pavement outside, where he squirmed in pain among the glittering shards of window.

Much of the brick front of the building was pushed into the office space, and half of the ceiling collapsed. I jumped from the truck, pulling the gun Ruby had given me from my waistband. I stepped through the dusty bricks and glass and into the ruined office. Dust still hung in the air, and pieces of the ceiling and roof were still falling. Chase rose up in the debris and turned to me. He was coated with chalky dust and particles of glass. His eyes were wide and wild and incredulous.

The other two men had their hands up, and they struggled to their feet.

I waded swiftly through the rubble to the goon nearest to me, pointed the gun directly at his face, and shouted, "Where's Arie? Where's my son, you sons of bitches?"

The two men glanced at each other. I clicked the safety off the gun.

"Answer me!" Rage and anger bubbled up inside of me, ready to overflow.

"Alison." Chase had raised his hands as well. "They don't know. They don't know what you're talking about. Okay? That's not why we're here right now."

"It's why I'm here." I didn't take my eyes off them. "I want to know why they were following him, and I want to know what they did to him. And I want to know right now."

There was an animal growl in my voice. I almost thought someone else was speaking—it surprised me. Something was surging inside me that wouldn't recede. I knew these men weren't responsible, but at the moment I didn't care. They had to know something. I had to start somewhere. And weren't they a part of it? The Agency? Voluntarily or not. They were the ones who stole my son from me.

And then it happened. One of the men laughed.

It was just a chuckle, but then he got a dopey grin on his face and he couldn't control it. Then the other man started laughing, too.

"Why are you laughing at me?" I shouted.

"Alison stop," Chase yelled.

But it was too late. My finger was already pulling the trigger.

I missed my target by several feet. The bullet went through the wall, but one of them fainted. The other man stayed frozen with his hands in the air. He stopped laughing.

"Oh, my God," I cried. I dropped the gun and collapsed to the floor. All the anger that had erupted within me suddenly changed to sorrow.

Chase scrambled from the dust to zip-tie the hands of both guards. I sat down and cried.

After Chase finished with the men, he wrapped his arms around me.

"I just want Arie back," I said.

"I know," Chase said. He stood up and began collecting the assault rifles that lay strewn in the chaos.

Woolly came running toward the building, flanked by Carlos with his hunting rifle. Woolly stepped into the building over the demolished window sill and surveyed the destruction.

"Interesting approach," he said, stroking his beard. He looked over at Chase and me on the ground. "What happened?"

Chase frowned and gestured vaguely at me, as if that were all the explanation the scene required. He laid the rifles into the bed of the truck and then shook the glass and plaster dust from his hair.

There was only one computer in the office. It lay beneath an overturned desk half-pinned by the bumper of the truck.

Chase told me to get in the truck and rest, and so I sat sheepishly in the driver's seat as the others set to work.

Chase questioned the guards while Woolly worked to extract the computer from the wreckage. He did his best to dust off the monitor and find a level place to turn it on, finally setting it on the fender of the truck. He got it plugged in and powered up, then sat on a chair with the keyboard in his lap, staring up at the monitor, which had numerous cracks running through it. It flickered and displayed crazy sprays of color. Only a few small shards of it actually worked properly.

Nevertheless, within five or ten minutes, Woolly announced, "I got it. The manifest for 8234-C. I think I can find the serum."

Ruby appeared, accompanied by Glen. They were winded and red-faced.

"We checked the north end," puffed Ruby, putting her pistol away. "No one else around."

"Yeah," said Chase. "These chumps say they're the only ones here, and they won't be rotated out for a couple days. We're safe, I think."

"Everyone okay?" asked Ruby.

Chase nodded.

Ruby glanced at me through the truck window—my red eyes and puffy face—but said nothing.

"Did someone cut the phone line?" she asked.

"I don't think that'll be necessary," Chase said. "We arrived quite suddenly."

"Good," she said. "We know where we're going yet?"

"Yeah," said Chase. "I think so. We might all be leaving in the Taurus, though, if that truck won't start."

Ruby assessed the Tacoma. Its grill was veiled in a web of twisted chain link. The crumpled hood was buried in plaster and mortar dust, and a wisp of steam rose from the radiator. A galvanized fence post lay uprooted and bent and dangling from one fender, and the pebbles of pulverized safety glass rattled around in the cab like sparkling popcorn. The windshield was crazed with silvery cracks, and the driver's-side door would no longer open.

"Well, Alison," said Ruby. "Will it go?"

I turned the key and the engine roared instantly to life.

Chase rolled his eyes. Carlos and Woolly looked at one another and nodded.

Ruby flashed a grin and said, "Let's go shopping."

*

Glen cut the lock to the warehouse and everyone but me scattered inside. Woolly rushed back to the truck with a crate labeled *MEDICAL SUPPLIES*. The others loaded up more—food, clothing, and other supplies and equipment they'd found. In fifteen minutes, the truck bed was full. Ruby tapped the hood of the truck. "Get her home, Al."

Chase was quiet as we drove back to the ranch house to pick up Gracie. I didn't know what to say. I hadn't killed anyone, but I'd tried. Ruby had said to never point the gun at someone unless I was ready to kill. And I'd been ready to kill. It scared me. Even though I'd asked for the gun, until that moment, I didn't know I could actually be capable of killing someone. Especially that way—someone defenseless, maybe even innocent. It more than scared me; it terrified me.

"I'm sorry," I said. "For back there."

He wouldn't look at me. "You could've killed someone, Al."

"I know. I know. I just—"

"You just let your emotions get in the way of your brain, is what you did."

"Yeah," I said. "I did."

Chase looked out the passenger side window. "You're outta the team. I'm telling Ruby to take you off."

"No, Chase, please. I'm sorry."

"You know this whole time you've only ever thought about yourself. You realize that? All the rest of us are out there risking our necks trying to make life better for everyone, and you're out there putting us all at risk just to get some revenge."

"That's not it," I protested. "It just—hurts so much, Chase. Please. I've learned my lesson. I was wrong."

"You have? What lesson is that?"

I recalled that moment when Chase sprinted to the office, and how I tried to protect him and how I would for any of the others on the team. It wasn't all selfishness. It really wasn't.

"That I've been going about it the wrong way. I'm not going to be able to find out what happened to Arie with a loaded gun. I'm going to have to plan it out and work with the rest of you. I need the team to get what I want, but I want to help the team get what we all need, too. I promise."

Chase scoffed. "You just don't get it, Alison. Your broken heart doesn't give you license to do whatever you want. You're not the only one who's ever been hurt."

I heard something in his voice. A vulnerability. A longing.

"You lost someone, didn't you?" I asked.

He didn't answer.

"You didn't lose somebody?"

"I did."

"Who?"

"I don't know. I can't remember."

"You've forgotten them already?"

"No." He waved his hand. "It was before the new year. Maybe a long time before."

"You remember something from before? How?"

"Al, no. It's not that. I don't remember them. I feel them. I miss them. I don't know who I lost but I know they're gone."

His words struck me inside and rang like a massive, brooding bell. It was a deep, mental chime that resonated.

"You ever feel like someone's missing?" he asked. "Someone you can't recall, but someone you know is gone?" He finally glanced over.

It took a while for me to answer. I was worried that my voice might crack.

"Yes."

CHAPTER 19

As we drove up to the old ranch house, I keyed the mic of the walkie-talkie.

"Little Lamb," I said. "This is Toyota Girl and Mountain Lion. Can you hear us?"

There was no response at first. I got ready to transmit again when we heard Gracie's voice. "Hi," she said.

Chase chuckled and looked over at me.

"Hi, Gracie," I said. "I mean—hi, Little Lamb. We're coming to get you, okay? See us coming?"

"Yeah," she said. Then she keyed the walkie-talkie again and added, "I'm bored. And hungry."

"Okay, sweetie," I said. "We'll be there in a few minutes. Sit tight."

She apparently had not gone into the house, but she was smiling when we pulled up. Chase smiled, too, and I was glad. I was still smothering under a cloud of regret and embarrassment, but it seemed to dissipate a little when we saw her stand and wave to us. Chase waved back.

Then, Chase and I climbed down from the cab and went straight to Gracie. She had delicate features and such tiny teeth—she reminded me of a kitten. You couldn't help but smile when she was around. No wonder Arie liked her. On the patch of ground where we'd left her, Gracie had constructed a small village of pebbles and twigs and grass. In another place, she'd used a stick to scratch tic-tac-toe games into a flat spot of dirt. All of the games had ended in cats' games.

"Let's get going, little girl," Chase called.

Gracie bounded into the truck and scrambled into the jump seat. Chase and I got in and buckled our belts.

"Why were you gone such a long time?" said Gracie.

Chase shook his head. "Hard to say."

Before I started the truck, I paused for a few moments. The way we were seated. Chase and I up front and Gracie behind—it felt so comfortable, so correct. I thought of how nice it would be to just drive, the three of us—just drive with nowhere to go and nothing to do. Maybe go to a beach or somewhere warm.

I glanced in the rear-view mirror and saw that Gracie's eyes were already closed, her arms wrapped around her lamb.

I began driving, but steered carefully so that I wouldn't disturb Gracie. She was so little. It was hard to imagine that she'd been surviving on her own for a year. And what had she done before that? I didn't remember our world from before, but I knew it had existed and I longed for it.

The drive back to Thrill Harbor took us through a small canyon. I steered onto the left-hand fork and the road took us higher, banking up and around a gentle curve. The sun was high in the sky now, and I squinted as it glared in through the windshield, which was hazy with grime and lined with silvery cracks.

The roads there in the foothills had been mostly devoid of cars; it was the highways and the closely packed residential streets in town where the failed evacuations had trapped so many vehicles, which now sat in impotent ruin on their rotting tires. That's why I immediately took notice when we rounded the broad bend and a massive black vehicle came into view just a few hundred yards ahead of us.

I stood on the brakes.

We flew forward hard, catching in the shoulder belts.

"Al, a little warning, jeeze" said Chase, rebounding into his seat.

He followed my gaze and saw it, too: an Agency troop carrier.

"Back up, back up, back up," Chase ordered, his hands flat on the dash.

"I know, I know," I said fumbling with the gear shift.

Gracie began to cry.

We'd come up on the troop carrier from behind; it was traveling in the same direction and it kept going, but I knew only one backward look by one Agency soldier was all it'd take for them to spot us.

I rammed the shift lever into reverse and got the Toyota backing up, and I turned in my seat to see out of the rear window of the cab. Chase watched out the front window, then behind, then front again. I caught sight of Gracie—her eyes were wide, her little mouth open.

The Agency vehicle disappeared around the bend and over the hill, but I kept backing up for another hundred yards.

"I've never seen a mounted patrol this far outside the boundaries," said Chase. "Must be something going on. Must be looking for something."

In the rear-view mirror, another angular and hulking form caught my eye. Another black troop carrier, this one coming up from behind.

"Us," I said, jamming in the clutch and putting the truck in first gear. "They're looking for us."

Gracie was crying steadily, her arms over her face and eyes.

CHAPTER 20

Chase shouted a series of crazed driving directions laced with more profanity than I'd expect even from him. He pointed, swiveled in his seat, looking forward and then back. He shouted some more. I floored the gas pedal and we raced back up the road, but then there was a new series of curses—from both of us, this time—when we realized the two Agency vehicles were converging on us.

"Off the road! Off the road!" hollered Chase. More cursing. More pointing and waving.

"Stop screaming at me!" I shouted back at him. "I can't drive while you're screaming."

"Get off this goddamn road!"

"And stop swearing at me!"

Chase bit down hard on his lip and held up a hand in an apparent apology. He looked behind us. Gracie shrunk down in her seat.

"Should I just stop?" I asked.

"No!" Gracie shouted.

"They've seen us," Chase said through bared teeth. "There is no place we can go but off the road."

"Where do I go?"

"There! There!" he blurted, pointing. "Off the road and down the hill."

I veered sharply left and the Toyota's suspension squawked noisily as we dropped off the highway and began to cross a down-sloping checkerboard of overgrown vacant lots. The grass was higher than the hood, and it hissed against the fenders. The dense clumps of sage and rabbit brush were topped with little caps of snow, and as we lurched over them, the snow exploded onto the hood and windshield.

I checked the mirror. The patrol vehicle proceeded along the road as though it might not follow. Chase spun around to see.

"Maybe they haven't seen us," he said with a maniacal little half-laugh. "How could they not see us?"

In the mirror, I saw the troop carrier slowing to a stop, and then the turret traversed until the massive barrel of the machine gun was trained on the truck.

"They've seen us," I assured him, hunching my shoulders to brace myself.

There came the rapid booming of heavy automatic gunfire. I felt it concussing in my inner ears, in my lungs. Chase cursed wildly. I pushed on the gas.

"Serpentine, Al, serpentine!" he said.

The gun ripped off another burst and I saw the rounds impact ahead of us in tall dirty plumes.

"Serpa what?" I screamed.

Chase grabbed the steering wheel and pulled it hard to the right. The truck swung right and all three of us were pitched over to the left. After a moment Chase pushed the wheel suddenly in the other direction and we leaned opposite. The truck's springs squawked and moaned.

"Serpentine," Chase hollered, letting go of the wheel. He made a snakelike motion with his hand. "Don't make it easy for them."

I snaked left again just as another deafening burst of gunfire erupted behind us, and the rounds kicked up dirt a mere yard away. I yanked the wheel hard right and they missed again.

Now just couple hundred yards behind us, the troop carrier left the road and followed our path down the face of the hill and into the sea of grass. I watched it in the mirror. The gun muzzle flashed and smoked and there came an unsettling delay as the sound caught up and another volley of rounds shrieked our way. This time the little Toyota shook with a series of sickening clanks and I knew we'd been hit. In the mirror, I saw the truck bed pitched up crazily and mangled, as if an enormous shark had chomped on it. The tailgate swung merrily from some remaining tendon of its hinge.

"Faster, Al!" yelled Chase. "Down the hill."

The incline got steeper and down we went, picking up speed and tearing through old fence lines and debris buried among the grass. Gracie screamed as though we were riding a derailing roller coaster. Clumps of brush whooshed past the busted-out driver's-side window, the last jagged fragments of which jounced on the floor of the cab.

It sounded as though the troop carrier was firing continuously now, and I heard it with my whole body. When my eyes darted to the mirror, I knew the Agency vehicles were gaining ground on us.

"The trees!" cried Chase.

With a flurry of pointing motions, Chase indicated a long row of old cottonwood trees at the edge of the lot ahead. "Head that way!"

The truck caught a low berm and went airborne for a second, then crashed down again. Gravel and dirt rattled against the undercarriage, and I fought the wheel to keep control as we thundered over the broken ground.

As we barreled down the slope and on toward the line of trees, I realized suddenly why Chase had steered me there. The thick trunks of the ancient trees were spaced far enough apart to allow the Toyota to pass, but definitely not the bulkier Agency vehicles. If we could crash through the wall of trees and brush, we might buy back some time and distance.

For a second or maybe two I narrowed my eyes in an attempt to calculate which two cottonwoods were best spaced to accommodate the width of the truck, but this was utterly futile in the time remaining before impact, and so I chose two at random and locked my elbows as I white-knuckled the wheel. The troop carrier kept firing.

We hit the tree line. There was a split-second roar of scraping metal, both of the side mirrors vanished in a leafy blur, and I knew we'd passed between.

But the wall of cottonwoods apparently marked the boundary where the gentler hillside ended and the cliff-like face of a much steeper slope began, and when we emerged from amidst the trees, the ground fell away beneath us, and the truck dove into an empty space. It was a drop of perhaps only twenty feet, but it seemed as though we descended for minutes upon minutes through open air. In the pit of my stomach I felt the sudden tickle of vertigo, such as when a car reaches the top of a steep hill and then plunges into the dip beyond.

At last the truck slammed to the steeply pitched ground blow. The windshield disintegrated in a startling shower of pebbled glass and we shot down the precipitous grade, bouncing from our seats so violently that not only did our heads strike the top of the cab but our shoulders, too. All I could do to keep the truck from veering too far and flipping into a rollover was squeeze the wheel in my two small fists.

*

When I came to, there was the taste of blood in my mouth and the smell of burning oil. But it was quiet. The engine had stopped and there were no sounds of gunfire or other vehicles. All of the windows of the truck were broken and the pebbles of glass were all around—down my shirt, in my hair. I looked over to see Chase slumped in his seat—his eyes shut, mouth open.

I turned and saw that the jump seat was empty. Gracie's little lamb was there on the floor, but Gracie was gone.

"Where's Gracie," I muttered.

Chase opened his eyes and blinked.

"Where's Gracie!" I clicked the button to release my seat belt and tore it off. I shouldered the door open. Deep gouges down the side of the miserable vehicle told how we'd had absolutely no space to spare between the tree trunks. And the tires were not only completely flat but had begun to unravel. The truck sat in the dirt on its rims in the furrow-like tracks it left, looking like it had exploded into its component pieces and then clumsily reassembled. It steamed and hissed.

"Gracie? Gracie!" I called.

I searched through the cottonwoods looking for her—desperation flooding my mind as I feared what may have happened.

Then I spotted a tiny bundle—so small—lying just beneath the line of trees we'd bashed through. It so easily could have been just a discarded jacket or bundle of clothes. But I knew instantly it was her.

I raced over. Blood covered her face. Her eyes were open—but fogged over and glassy. Already the skin around her mouth had turned blue.

Dead.

I screamed and Chase was suddenly beside me.

"You've got to save her," I said, tugging furiously at his jacket. "Please, please, please. You've got to."

He knelt beside her, but then looked back at me. His eyes were wet.

"No," I cried. "Do CPR. Do something. She can't be gone. No."

He turned back to her and gently picked her up—she was limp. Like a doll. And so tiny in his arms.

He looked like he might say something, but then his chin crumpled and he pressed his lips together to keep from sobbing.

I wanted to die. It hurt so much—seeing Gracie's broken body and Chase's sorrow. It was more than I could bear. All that had happened—it was too much. For as little as I knew Gracie, I loved her. Chased loved her. We all did. And now she was gone.

"This is my fault," I said.

Chase shook his head. "No."

But I knew it was. Insisting that Gracie come along, pulling the gun on the Agency Officers, driving the car off a cliff—I had killed Gracie. I had killed her. A living angel of a girl.

*

It was dusk by the time Chase finished digging the grave. We had both cried on and off as he worked. Our eyes and noses were red. We didn't talk much at all. I didn't feel real. I felt like an outsider watching a horrible scene take place.

We had no shovel and so Chase had loosened the soil with his knife and then cleared it away using an old board he found in the truck.

"It's not very deep," he said.

"It'll be okay," I said.

He gingerly laid her body in the grave and covered it with her blanket.

In the weak sunlight, he used the board to push the soil back into the grave. It felt wrong to be covering her up that way.

Once Gracie was buried, Chase and I collected a few dozen large stones to cover over the grave.

"I feel like we should say something," I said.

"What is there to say?" Chase asked as he stared at the pile of stones.

What was there to say? I couldn't make sense of it. Losing my memories, Arie, and now Gracie. Why? Why was it happening?

We opened the boxes we had stolen from the Agency and box after box was filled with broken glass—the life-saving serum seeped out. Not even one dose had survived the chase. And so then it was all for nothing.

"I should have stopped when we saw the Agency vehicles," I said.

Chase shook his head almost imperceptibly.

"She'd still be alive then," I said.

"We'd have been arrested," Chase said. "And with all that stuff in the back, we'd almost surely been shot."

"But she'd be alive."

Chase swallowed hard. "You don't know that."

Rewind. Rewind. Nothing could fix this. Nothing. I considered the trajectory that had taken us to this moment and wondered where a change could have been made, where things could have been altered. There were so many forks in the road, so many chances. If only I'd known.

I was disgusted with myself. What kind of person was I? I'd failed Arie. I'd failed Gracie. I'd failed Chase and all the others. What was I good for? Nothing.

Chase got out his binoculars again and scanned the darkness. I sat in the rubble watching him.

"We should go," he said, lowering the binoculars. "They went to the bottom of the foothills. Probably looking for us down there, waiting for us. But they'll make their way up here, eventually."

Chase got to his feet and slapped the dust from the seat of his pants. "Let's get moving. Find someplace to bed down."

We walked down through the foothills toward town, but we found no homes. Soon the temperature dropped until the nightly hoarfrost appeared on everything, and so we settled for a small brick pump house in a ravine by a road. It had one door and two small windows, and there was nothing inside but an electric pump with its water pipes, which came up through the floor and exited through the back wall. I looked around. It was bleak and dusty but it was well sheltered from the cold, and there was just enough room for us to lie down.

"Can we make a fire?" I asked.

"Yeah," said Chase. "A little one won't hurt."

We gathered up some tinder and a few armfuls of deadfall. Chase produced a lighter and built a small fire beneath a window that swung open. In a few minutes the small space grew reasonably warm. I lay down with my head on my pack. Chase sat with his back against the wall, and his stretched-out legs almost reached me across the tiny room.

"Hungry?" he asked.

"No," I said.

His face was ruddy and somber in the firelight. "I'm going to miss her," he said.

"I know," I said. "Me too."

189

Chase sniffed and looked down. "Won't matter in a few months. We'll just forget."

I sat up. "What do you mean? What about the other serum?"

"Well, you're assuming that Ruby and the others managed to get away with their load of serum, and you're further assuming that it won't wipe our memories. And on top of that, you're assuming that I'm willing to take it."

"If you're not even going to take it, then why are you working with Ruby and the rest?"

He shrugged. "That was before."

"So you'll go back to the Agency? Forget again?"

"You want me to remember this?"

"We need our memories to be ourselves. And we need your memories. This is how you want to deal with it? Let them poison you again and erase anyone you've ever loved? Erase Gracie?" I could hear the angry growl in my own voice.

I'd heard somewhere that anger wasn't a primary emotion—that it was always cover for some other emotion—like fear or sadness—and I knew in my case it was both.

"Why do you care?" asked Chase. "Why are you angry with me?"

"It's fine, Chase. Go ahead and start the new year with none of your memories. But what about what you know? What you've learned?"

He sighed. Then he shrugged. "I apparently woke up with the ability to take care of myself. I assume that's how I'll wake up next time."

"Maybe you could use what you know now to help other people."

"How could I possibly use any of this to help other

people? How does seeing that little girl's face in my mind make one damn difference?"

"Chase, if we can't remember anything, then what's the point? All we have is our memories. And even when they're taken from us, we feel the people we've lost. You said it yourself. You lost someone—you don't know who but you miss them."

"I want to live peacefully more than I want to remember," he said.

"Not me. I'd rather die than take that serum again. And you can't forget anyway. You'll always miss Gracie, even if you can't remember her. You know that, right?"

He looked down at the fire and said nothing.

"I can't just give away everything I know again," I said. My voice caught and hitched. "I can't forget—"

"Them," he said.

We looked at each other across the fire for a while. It snapped and fumed.

"Hell, I might even want to remember you," I said. "But I can't keep letting them take everything away from me."

We were quiet then. After a while we lay down with our backs to the fire. I took off my coat and draped it over myself for a blanket, then dozed a little. Chase shifted on the concrete.

"Chase?" I said.

"Yeah." His voice was oddly clear in the small, quiet room.

"Tell me the truth. Would you really be okay if you forgot?"

"No, Al. I'm starting to think it'd be a big mistake to forget any of this."

CHAPTER 21

In the morning we began the trek back to the amusement park. It was far enough that we agreed it'd take most of the day to make it back—maybe two. But we could drink from the river, and we both had a little food in our packs. Chase had his radio, but the battery was more than half expended.

He radioed Ruby as we walked and told her about Gracie.

"Dammit," Ruby had said. That was all. We figured she turned off her radio after that. I could picture the rest of them hearing the news and the gloominess that would permeate the space. The anger and sadness and regret they would feel and that we still felt. Woolly, Carlos, even Glen—we all adored that little girl.

I suspected they'd blame me, and I deserved it. Over their objections, I'd put her in harm's way. I knew I could never make it up to them. It made my heart heavy.

What had happened changed things between Chase and me, and it was the last thing I would have expected. I thought he'd want nothing to do with me, but instead it seemed to make us closer. His opinion was that Gracie's death was a consequence of the toxic, dysfunctional world she found herself in. A hundred different perils awaited a child like Gracie in this world—

being thrown from the truck was simply the one that claimed her.

And passing through that heartbreak together— placing her in that shallow grave and then covering her with dirt—was something few others would be able to understand. He held my hand as we walked, helping me over fences and jumping across creeks.

We had a new bond. It was a sad one, but it was strongly forged—as long we remembered.

Still, we didn't speak as we walked back, almost as though we were carrying out a silent vigil in memory of little Gracie.

The trees along the path edged closer in, so Chase walked behind me, occasionally bumping into me.

"I can't get over thinking about it," Chase finally said.

"I know," I said. "I'm sorry."

"Is this how it was? When you lost your son?"

I nodded.

"Does it get better?"

"No," I answered honestly. "You just make room for it."

"You're a good person, Alison. You're nice. Everyone knows that. Makes me want to be a little nicer, too."

I didn't feel nice. Not after all that had happened. Not after the poisons that had seeped into me—rage, vengeance, selfishness.

"I don't blame you," said Chase. It was almost like he was reading my thoughts. "And I mean that."

The trees began to thin, allowing the sun to shine through. It warmed our faces. The air was crisp and fresh. The ground was soft with wet leaves and bark.

"I think we want to head up there, cross the bluff, then back down into town," said Chase.

I nodded, and we went. The sun stood high in the sky now, and it grew warm. Winter birds darted among the bare branches of the trees, fluttering in petty disputes over the sparse forage.

We crossed the river over a rotting footbridge, then pressed through a thicket of Russian olive. When we came through, we found ourselves at the edge of an enormous meadow of low, gently rolling mounds. With only patches of snow remaining, the meadow was grown with tall, bronze-colored grass that seemed to glow in the sunshine. Off in the distance a herd of doe deer raised their heads from grazing and watched us.

"Wow," I said. "Pretty."

The only signs I could see that people had ever been there were on the far edge of the expanse, where a few yellow-orange bulldozers and some trucks stood idle in the otherwise pastoral setting, and even the machines were grown around with weeds and saplings. It was some abandoned excavation now almost obliterated by nature. I walked into the waist-high grass and let the sun warm my face.

"Al," said Chase from somewhere behind me. "Hold up a sec."

I turned. Chase had stopped. His hands were on his hips, and he looked at the ground with a frown. He took a few steps, kicked at something.

"What is it?" I asked. "What's wrong?"

He bent down and wrested something from the soft ground. It was a sneaker.

I chuckled. It was just so random. "What's that doing here?"

His eyes had darkened and his lips were pressed into a hard line. "On second thought, let's go back and follow the river down," he said.

"Back that way?" I asked as I walked his way. "Won't that take forever? And it'll take us closer to the highway. There could be patrols."

"It's just—"

That is when I saw it. A human arm, and a hand. Just bones pressed into the earth and almost obscured by the grass. There were a few shreds of shirt sleeve, and a wristwatch, its metal parts covered with green and white scales and corrosion, loosely circling the bleached white wrist.

Then I looked across the meadow, noticing for the first time that the rolling mounds were orderly, evenly spaced.

"What is this place?" I said.

"Let's go back."

I walked on. The meadow whispered as wind shushed through the blades of grass.

"Al, really," said Chase.

The ground was littered with tattered and half-buried artifacts. Bits of clothing, a pair of crushed eyeglasses, purses. And the shoes—hundreds of shoes. There were bones, of course, showing whitely in the sun. Femurs, ribs, the round caps of skulls—all of them disarticulated and scattered. My stomach twisted.

We came to one of the mounds. It was only twelve feet tall. I crested it and counted ten more ahead in long rows. I raced over them with an urgent curiosity. The little herd of grazing deer fled into the tree line at my coming. Across the meadow there was another row of the mounds, and another beyond.

Chase followed me, but at a distance.

Then I reached the bulldozers and saw what they had excavated years ago. The contours of the grim work site were softened by erosion and the prolific grass, but it wasn't hard to figure out. A shallow, empty trench and beside it a pile of pushed-up earth—bulldozers still standing by to push it back into place. The trench was thirty or forty feet wide and its length was three times that.

On the near side of the trench the grass grew unevenly. I knew what I would find there, but I had to know.

The remains of hundreds of people, lined up and stacked. Disturbed now by scavengers and the elements, but it had once been a wall of corpses awaiting interment in hasty, industrial graves, the final abandoned project of the society that was. The skeletons lay intermingled now, each bone belonging to all. Weeds grew up through eye sockets and between the startling white ribs, and all picked clean—first by birds and mammals, and finally by maggots and beetles and ants. So many skulls they formed a whited cobblestone path. So many toes and foot bones they lay piled like reefs of gravel. Child-sized skeletons in once-brightly colored coats were cradled in between the adults. Decaying clothing melted over them all, like dripping rags.

Arie and I had visited their houses, ransacked their belongings. Street after street, block after block. And I'd wondered where the people had gone to. I looked back at the mounds I had crossed and the field of human debris beyond that—the remains of those who were dumped with even less care.

They were here. At last I'd found them.

I'd often envisioned them outside somewhere. Evacuated past the Zone boundaries, living lives that were at least somewhat normal and happy. And remembering. How lucky they were, I'd think. But they never got out. The dead lay here by the tens of thousands, so many of them that the toil of burying them had surely turned desperate and sloppy and enormously repugnant to those who were left to do it. And the open trench and pile of unburied dead was a final testament that it was a job that ultimately went unfinished.

The rest of us, living in miserable circumstances without memories and only little hope of something better—it turns out, we were the lucky ones.

It wasn't the first time I'd seen a person so long dead. Sometimes Arie and I would creep into an abandoned house and the putrid, musty scent of death would still linger delicately inside. People who hadn't been found or processed. Once we saw the body of a man from the front window of his bungalow, before we had even tried the door knob. He was desiccated, eyeless, his skin a dusky gray, black mouth agape. His blond hair was standing on end—the shocking result of the way his scalp had shrunk and hardened and he slowly mummified.

The Agency had drilled us on the dangers of approaching the corpses—because of the pandemic and other possible infection. And so we'd pull the door shut and back away if we knew there were dead inside.

And we'd seen those who died much more recently. The chip-rippers and squatters who decided to go it alone without the Agency's help and died outside the Zones. The virus likely got most of them, but there were other causes. Starvation, exposure, murder—the death who stalked us wore a hundred faces.

Some of the dead, I often suspected, simply had insufficient purpose to live. No one can predict the future, but the ability to recall the past can be a strong shield against the vicious blows of future uncertainty. Without that awareness, without any idea of who they'd been, the amnesiac pandemic survivors labored under the wild and shifting burden of the present moment, trapped in that instant, without memories or wisdom to look back on, and no hope to look forward to. Little surprise then that some ended their own lives and others simply collapsed in the street without apparent cause.

And no wonder the living skirted those unfortunate fallen until the hazmat team arrived to sweep them up and carry them away like spilled garbage.

In fact, you could say it had become commonplace in this world to pass by the dead and dying without the wherewithal to mourn or ask after them. But even that pathetic existence hadn't prepared me for the evidence of death we saw there in the meadow. The sheer scale of it. And the truth of it—for the first time I knew the pandemic was something actual. Not something abstract or falsified. It wasn't propaganda or even something historical. Here was a journal of the plague written in an alphabet of bones. Acres of them. The Agency might have been stealing our memories for some sinister purpose, but that did not mean we hadn't died by the thousands and millions before they took over. How many more graves like this must there be?

Who were they, really? A toddler running through a sprinkler, a teenager driving his first car, an elderly couple sharing a sunset.

Among these bones, upon which fell both sun and snow, were there people I once knew? Or loved?

All at once, the fragility of not just my own life and the people I knew but that of all humanity weighed on me with such force that I grew dizzy, and could only breathe in gasps.

Chase joined me at my side; his face bleak and arms folded.

"So, what they told us is true." I said.

Chase stared at the ground.

"You've been here before?" I asked.

"Not here," he said. "There are others."

"So many."

Without a word, Chase wrapped his arms around me, tucking my head beneath his chin, and we stood there a long time—the only two people alive.

CHAPTER 22

It was night again by the time we made it back to Thrill Harbor. The great spokes of the Sky Dreamer masked the sea of stars in the moonless night. We climbed over the barricades in the icy gloom and walked. The funhouse door was a huge clown's face with a mouth frozen in a grotesque laugh which loomed darkly as we passed by.

Soon we reached the tunnel under the Ferris wheel, where I'd first met Glen, and my throat tightened involuntarily. Despite the more-or-less favorable conclusion to that encounter, I all at once recalled the fear that gripped me that day as he stepped from the shadows and put his hands on me. I looked up and saw Chase getting ahead of me and so I quickened my pace.

It had been sunny that day. The icy mud in the bottom of the tunnel must have melted and then refrozen in the night, because the ground was now as smooth and hard as an ice rink. As I walked faster to catch Chase, my boot lost its grip and I fell—the kind of a fall that begins with pin-wheeling arms and a frantic frictionless shuffle, then continues with a feet-in-the-air freefall, and ends with the dull thud of landing squarely on the back with a smart crack to the skull. Electric sparks strobed for an instant behind my eyelids.

I wasn't sure if Chase had heard my head bang on the ice or the breathless "oof" I emitted, but he stopped and turned back.

"Are you okay?" he asked.

I thought about the question for a few seconds.

"Yeah," I croaked.

"You sure?"

I thought about it.

"No," I sighed.

He chuckled.

"I'll help you up."

I heard him moving toward me and so I lay there on my back and waited.

"You really hurt?" He knelt by me.

"I don't think so." I propped myself on one elbow. "Just hurts."

"Hit your head?"

"Uh huh."

"Well, hang on," he said. "Stay still a sec."

He got out his flashlight and clicked it on. I touched the back of my head, squinting at the sudden brightness.

"I don't see any blood," said Chase. "But as your doctor I'm afraid I must recommend that you not try out for the Ice Capades this year."

"Just help me up," I said, grabbing at him feebly.

"Wait a sec. Hold still. Jeeze." He took off his jacket, rolled it up, and set it under my head. Then he shined the flashlight into my eyes, first one and then the other, gently holding my eyelids open with his fingers.

"Feel sick?" he asked. "Nauseous?"

"You mean nauseated," I corrected.

He laughed. It was a curt guffaw, but was good to hear even that much laughter. "Do you feel nauseated?" he corrected.

I took a deep breath and closed my eyes. "I guess not."

"Okay. Let's get you up."

He stood, gripped my forearm, and leaned back to haul me up. I was partway upright when without warning Chase's feet slipped and he repeated my pin wheeling spill onto the ice. He landed on his back and I landed again on mine. For a long moment we lay there on our backs and neither of us said anything.

"You all right?" I asked after a minute.

"Yeah," said Chase.

"You sure?"

"No," he sighed.

I laughed, then Chase laughed. And we kept laughing for a while. It was as though my body could take no more sadness, and though it really wasn't that funny, I found I couldn't stop. And it was the first time I could remember having really laughed since I'd been with Arie. It was as though I'd been denying myself the privilege of smiles and laughter, and through that one tiny rupture it came pouring out like a lake through the breach in a burst dam. Tears filled my eyes, I held my sides, and soon I hadn't enough air to breathe.

When I finally recovered, I looked at over at Chase. His little flashlight had bounced away from him and it lit part of the tunnel wall with its sideways-shining beam. Chase sat on his butt watching me, his folded arms resting on his knees.

"Are you quite finished?" he asked with a weary smile.

"Oh god." I wiped my eyes and took several deep breaths. "Yeah," I chuckled. "I'm finished. But if it's all right with you, please don't try to help me anymore."

As I got to my feet on the slippery ground, I saw the

graffiti painted in red, which I'd seen the first day I'd come to the amusement park to find Ruby. My eyes absently scanned the crazy lettering, but then locked onto the large symbol sprayed nearby in the same color paint.

It was the figure of a human skull combined with the face of a clock on the forehead.

Chase must have noticed the change in my expression because he stood hastily and came to my side.

"Al?"

"Look!" I cried, pointing.

He read the words and stepped forward.

"Okay," said Chase, squinting at the crazy writing. "Boats against the current. Great Gatsby. So?"

"The skull!" I said. "That's the skull!"

He bent down and picked up the flashlight, then shined it directly on the symbol. "Yeah. I've seen this. Where have I seen this?"

I tore Arie's coded notebook from my backpack and nearly shoved it into Chase's face.

Chase shined the flashlight beam on the red cover of the notebook, then the tunnel wall, and back again.

"I'll be damned," he said.

My spine tingled in the damp darkness of the tunnel, and I shivered. For a moment, it was as though Arie had joined us in the tunnel, or we had joined him. I pictured him standing there painting the letters with spray cans he'd found somewhere, crouching and lifting himself onto tiptoes to elongate the letters.

"All these times I've come through here," said Chase. "I don't think I'd ever really looked at that."

"Wait," I said. My heart hammered in my chest. Blood roared in my ears. I grabbed Chase by the sleeve of his jacket to steady myself. "Wait."

He cradled my elbows and frowned. "What? What?"

I spoke slowly. "What did you say about The Great Gatsby?"

He swept the beam of his light across the wall and the red letters.

"Boats against the current," he said, suddenly unsure of himself. "That's—a line from *The Great Gatsby*. The last line. Isn't it?"

"Oh, no!"

"What?" cried Chase. I felt as though I might collapse.

"That's the key," I said. "*The Great Gatsby*. The code. The key. I have it. It's at my house." I let go of Chase and stuffed the notebook into my backpack. Then I turned back and started for the mouth of the tunnel, nearly slipping as I slung the pack onto my back again.

"I have to go. I have to go right now."

"Hold on," he said. "I'll go with you. Al, wait up. Wherever it is you need to be off to, I'll help."

Just then Chase's radio squawked.

"Mountain Lion, where the hell are you?" asked Ruby.

Chase looked at the radio.

"You need to be with them," I said. "They're in mourning. I can get the book on my own."

Chase pressed his lips together, but then he nodded.

It felt like we needed to be together—all of us—after we'd lost so much. But discovering what could possibly be the key to Arie's secret diary held an immediacy I couldn't avoid. I'd been given the chance again to talk to him, and I couldn't turn down that chance for anything. The red paint screamed out on the wall of the tunnel like a neon sign.

"I'll get the book, and I'll come right back," I told

him. "Tell them all how sorry I am."

I found my bike at the park entrance and I hurriedly unlocked it and then I was off. I stood up on the pedals and rode fast toward home in the frigid night. The icy air rushing across my face made my eyes water, and my hands ached and then turned numb with cold, but I was warm inside from the mixture of hope and adrenaline.

At the time, I didn't know the significance of my decision to leave Chase there in the tunnel. I didn't know that it would change everything.

CHAPTER 23

I biked faster than I ever had before. An urgency pressed on my mind, an excitement. Had I ever in the past nine or ten months been so excited? My legs burned and then they ached, but I only pedaled harder.

I knew just where to find the book. It was in Arie's room. A bluish book cover with a painting of a woman's face and an amusement park. While I rode, I imagined holding it in my hands, sitting on the bed with it and Arie's notebook. Finding out, at last, the secret words that could be the key to understanding his disappearance or at the very least knowing him more—unearthing another layer of my son who already in my mind was so complex and beautiful. I needed to hear his words in my mind. I needed it.

My hands shook as I ditched the bike in the front yard without locking it, and I scrambled up the porch steps and into the house.

I raced up the stairs and into Arie's bedroom, which was still in disarray from my earlier frantic searching. But I found the messy pile of books which I'd removed from his book shelf. I knelt and sorted through them. I knew what I was looking for, exactly what I was looking for. Blue cover. Woman's face. Amusement park.

But it wasn't there.

Perhaps I'd just missed it. I forced myself to slow down, to pick up the books one at a time. I arranged them in a neat pile, double checked, triple checked.

But it wasn't there.

After taking a few breaths, deliberately slowed down. I tried to calm myself. It was here somewhere. It had to be.

"Okay, just breathe for a sec," I told myself.

My eyes surveyed the room. There was the desk, the bed, the dresser. The books had been there. I'd searched through them before finding Arie's notebook and then—

A sudden sick feeling seeped into my stomach.

I hadn't given the book to Donna, had I? When I'd gone to get more notebooks—was it one of the books I'd gathered up for her?

It was. It had to be.

I closed my eyes trying to bring myself back to that moment. I had so few memories, surely I could remember. My mind took me back that day—how was it that it seemed so long ago? I remembered the heavy sadness, the way my heart felt like lead, and my urgent need for more notebooks and pens. And yes, there was Donna with her glasses and big eyes and all her cats. I'd handed her the book with several others. I'd handed her the key to unlocking everything.

I cursed myself and grabbed my backpack from the bed. It'd take nearly twenty minutes to get to Donna's trailer. Every minute I had to wait was agony.

"God, please let her still have it."

I raced back down the stairs, nearly stumbling, and then jumping down the last three steps all together.

I had no idea they were there, waiting for me.

Maybe it was because I was so focused on getting the

book that I didn't hear them.

Maybe it was because I was breathless and my heart was pounding.

Maybe they'd just been very quiet.

When I opened the front door, I was greeted by six Agency men with their guns trained on me.

Standing behind them was Gary Gosford, looking grim-faced and angry.

"Hi, Alison," he said.

CHAPTER 24

We sat on opposite sides of my couch—Gary and me.

Gary had folded his arms and he scowled deeply. I sat impassively. Gary could have one of his goons shoot me in the head and leave me there in my living room, and all I was able to think of was where my copy of *The Great Gatsby* might be.

Two Agency goons stood guard at the entrance to the living room. They were young—early twenties, not much older than Arie—but they looked hardened and mean, like the type that would throw rocks at a cat for laughs. Or maybe I only thought they looked that way because they were here in my house, uninvited, with guns. The other goons were elsewhere in the house, maybe even stationed outside. One of them had taken my backpack and with it Arie's notebook.

"I'm hurt that you would lie to me, Alison," said Gary. "I thought we were friends."

I didn't answer. I wasn't sure what he knew or why he was there. It was better to stay quiet than to accidentally reveal too much.

I'd seen people beaten by goons, get dragged away. I'd heard that people were sometimes interrogated, seemingly at random. And I knew people who vanished and never showed up again. I tried to keep my face from showing emotion, but my heart began to beat so hard I could feel it in my throat.

Gary stood up. He held his hands behind his back and paced around the room—though there wasn't much room for pacing—as if deep in thought.

"It's funny," Gary said, "there are some people who, no matter how many chances we give them, no matter how many times we erase their memories, they still turn out the same way. Bad apples. Bad seeds."

I looked up at him. It was the first time I'd heard any Agency man comment on our memory loss as something other than a side effect of the serum. He'd said, "we erase their memories."

"I'm not talking about you, of course," Gary continued. He didn't look at me as he said this. He walked with his chin up, affecting a countenance of authority. "You just fell in with a bad crowd. They're like a disease, you know? They infect others—good people, like you. God knows we've tried to be humane, given them more chances than they deserve. But we can't tolerate it anymore. They're a cancer, and they need to be removed."

I wasn't entirely sure who or what Gary was talking about. Ruby and Chase and the others, I assumed? But was he referring to others that I maybe didn't even know about? Had Ruby been working against the Agency all along? Year after year? How could they fall into the same roles without their memories? Could it be what Arie thought? Did he know? Did he know that we still had all our memories and somewhere, unconsciously, they still influenced our actions?

Gary stopped pacing and looked at me. "I forgive you," he said. His voice was earnest and steady.

"Personally, I mean. I forgive you. And I don't blame you for lying to me. In fact, I haven't been completely honest with you, either."

There was a clock in the living room and as Gary paused for a moment, I heard it ticking. It was solar-powered, a nice little clock that Arie had found in the neighborhoods. And it had kept great time all the while Arie and I had been together, but usually the sound it made was nearly imperceptible. Now it seemed as loud as a drumbeat. Tick, tick, tick.

"I know you think I'm just an Agency supervisor. You call us 'goons'." He smiled bitterly but didn't look at me.

I watched him, my heart still pounding. The clock went tick, tick, tick.

"I'm actually a recruiter for Lotus."

Now I was sure I didn't know what he was talking about.

"Have you heard of Lotus? The Lotus Project?" He looked my way. "Ring any bells?"

I shook my head.

"Good. That's as it should be. Lotus is a very special program that is meant to improve things for everyone. We know things are bad. Things are bad for people here in gen-pop and they're bad in other places, too. And we all want to make it better. Even your friends, the bad seeds—they think they're fighting to make things better. Right?"

I didn't answer.

Gary smiled his bitter smile, then continued. "The difference between Lotus and your pals running amok outside Zone boundaries is that Lotus will succeed because only the brightest and most highly skilled are invited to participate."

I fought to keep myself from responding, fought to keep my expression neutral, but Gary had certainly gotten my attention. What was he talking about?

He sat on the couch again, but this time very close to me, so close that our legs were touching. He grabbed my hand.

"Arie is very, very smart. You know that, don't you?"

Is?

Not *was*.

I felt the rage again, the rage that made me pull the trigger of a gun I'd pointed at a person. It was an animal savagery born from desperation and helplessness. It bloomed suddenly like some brutal flower in my heart. I felt as though I could pounce on Gary and begin to pull him apart like a plastic doll. This talk of a mysterious program and recruitment—it made a certain sense in the rational recesses of my mind. Some secret he'd kept from the wretched members of gen-pop—it was an answer to lots of questions I'd carried around for the last year. But at that moment, my mind had space for one thought, one word: *is*.

It was a word that meant my doom.

Gary stopped speaking and examined the sleeve of his coat. A thread had come loose from the buttonhole on the cuff. He frowned at it for a moment before pinching it between his fingers and plucking it sharply away. Then he stood again and cleared his throat.

"You and your companions down in that filthy amusement park have committed treason, Alison. Unless I intervene, you'll be shot. Summarily. No questions, no trial, nothing."

Gary blinked down at me, searching for any response, any sign I might give. I knew where this was going now, but I made no signal. The clocked ticked.

"But because this is your first offense," said Gary, "and because I personally know you to be a law-abiding member of our society, I'm going to make you a deal."

I swallowed hard. I couldn't help it. I knew what he was about to say, and it was something I both longed and dreaded to hear.

He chuckled. "Yeah. We know they're down in that neighborhood. Down in some little lair. I've got almost a hundred armed men ready to storm the place. They're ready to burn the entire area to the ground. But I know they're clever, these friends of yours. If I send my men in, I just know your friends are going to make a lot of trouble. There'll be casualties, and your friends could slip away, and that won't look good on my record. Plus, I need to know what they know, what they've got planned, what they've already done. They've got to be questioned. I need this to be a clean incision, Alison."

I don't know why I kept listening. I knew exactly what he was thinking.

"You could help," said Gary. "Tell me exactly where they are. I mean exactly. And if you do, the Agency will forgive you for your crimes."

I thought about it. Even though I knew I could never accept the offer, I thought about it. Gary was right— Ruby and the others were clever. They'd set up their operation and had reached the verge of freeing themselves from the Agency, all in one year. Of course, they had secret passages, traps, and who could say what else. They were heavily armed and highly motivated. And they knew the park inside and out. They could make so much trouble. They could hold out for a week or maybe more. Or they could fade into the woods with their serum and take up the fight somewhere else, on their own terms, raiding and running and then fading into the woods again. Gary really did need me.

"I won't help you," I said.

Gary nodded. "I understand. And I actually admire your loyalty. It's a quality I value highly. You know, loyalty is all I ever wanted from you and Arie. I always had your best interest in mind."

"I'm sorry. I can't turn them in just to save myself."

"They'll torture you before they execute you, Alison," said Gary. "They'll torture it out of you."

"You mean you'll torture it out of me."

Gary inhaled abruptly. "Alison, I'm thinking only about—"

"Yourself. You're thinking of yourself. I don't know what's going on with your project or why you took Arie, but I see it now—it was you all along. That's why you didn't come to help when I told them your name. That's why you were following Arie and me."

Gary shook his head.

"And that's why you poisoned Arie. It was the peanut butter, wasn't it? You're evil."

Gary paused. He looked at the floor and took some deep breaths. "As I was saying. You're loyal to your friends," he said, stammering a bit. "I can understand that. But I'm sure you've figured out by now that Arie isn't dead. Are you loyal to him? Tell me where your little team is and I will take you to him tonight."

And there it was. I should have been happy. I would have given almost anything to see Arie again. And I actually trusted Gary's offer—I believed that he would let me see Arie if I cooperated. But as Gary stood over me there in my living room, I resigned myself to never seeing Arie again.

"Okay, Gary," I said. "I accept."

CHAPTER 25

They handcuffed me and wedged me between two armed goons in the back seat of a black Crown Victoria. My neighbors watched from their windows. A few came out onto their porches. The same people who'd come out of their houses to watch me drive around in the jacked-up Tacoma now watched with the same slack-jawed amazement as a detachment of goons stuffed me into a very different automobile to take me away forever.

Gary sat in the front passenger seat and another goon did the driving. We set out for Thrill Harbor with two troop carriers following.

Arie was alive. Of course he was. I was his mother, and I'd known all along. So, why did I feel such relief and happiness? Why did I need Gary to confirm what I already knew?

Maybe it was like our memory loss—somewhere in my heart I'd known I had a son, but someone from the Agency had to remind me of that. It had already been real in my heart, but it had to be made real in my mind. Likewise, my heart knew Arie was alive, but I needed Gary to say the word "is" so that my mind knew it, too.

And when I knew with both my heart and mind, I realized there was only one path for me to follow. Yes, I could see Arie again if I wanted to—all I had to do was betray the only friends I had in the entire world. All I had to do to get what I wanted was sell out five considerate and selfless human beings to be summarily executed.

We drove along the streets and the highway, edging and swerving past the derelict cars. I saw the Ferris wheel looming in the distance. That is where I'd meet my end. I'd resigned myself to my fate, but that didn't keep my stomach from churning like a washing machine.

"I feel sick," I said.

Gary pressed a button and the rear windows opened an inch or so.

Cool air flooded into the car.

"How's that?" said Gary with surprising sincerity. "Better?"

It wasn't better.

Gary explained his plan to the goon who was driving. "Bill, you'll take the two squads from the APCs and follow us into the amusement park. Twelve men should be enough if we've got a lock on their location. We'll have the others in reserve in case things go south."

The driver nodded.

Gary swiveled in his seat to face me and the two goons who flanked me in the back seat.

"Oberman, Manwaring," he said. "I want you two with me and the prisoner at all times. Don't let her out of your sight. If she tries to run, shoot her."

The goons nodded, but I had no plans to run anywhere.

"No offense, Alison," said Gary. "I just need this to go smoothly."

"It's fine," I replied.

"We'll go in dark and quiet," said Gary to the goons. "As soon as the prisoner gives us the location, Oberman and Manwaring will escort me and the prisoner back here until the op is complete.

Bill and the two goons grunted their acknowledgment.

"Alison, I'm a man of my word—that's when I'll take you to Arie."

I nodded.

We drove on.

As we got closer to the amusement park, a strange sense of calm and contentment welled up inside me. With me out of the equation, I knew Ruby and her team would continue their work and continue fighting. Serum or no serum, memories or no memories, they would find a way. And Arie? Gary was right about him. He was very, very smart. Smarter than me, I'd come to learn, and certainly much smarter than Gary. I didn't know where he was or if they'd taken his memories or if he was a prisoner somewhere, but I knew he'd continue his work, too—in whatever form that might take.

When I accepted Gary's amnesty bargain, I'd offered to tell him exactly where Ruby's team was holed up. I told him I'd draw him a detailed map.

But he said, "No, no, Alison. You're not getting off that easily. You're taking us there. In person. Once we have them in custody, you'll see Arie."

I knew Gary would want me to be there, not just to ensure I didn't trick him somehow, but also to parade me in front of Ruby and the others like a Judas.

I not only knew he'd take me personally to the park, I'd counted on it. It was the only way my plan would even work.

"You'll want to kill all your lights now," I said as we approached the turnoff to the Thrill Harbor parking lot complex. "They're probably asleep by now, but with all the excitement lately they'll be standing watch. One of them is probably out walking a patrol, too. If they even think someone's coming for them, they'll vanish."

Bill turned to Gary.

"Do it," said Gary.

Bill turned off the Crown Vic's headlights, then radioed the troop carriers and told them to do the same.

Gary turned his head and gave me a commendatory nod.

Soon the big Crown Vic with its troop carrier escorts rolled up to the vast and empty Thrill Harbor parking lots. We parked on the outer edge of the lot, farthest from the park entrance. We were perhaps a mile from the haunted house and the soldiers moved like cats in the darkness—if Ruby and the others were keeping watch, they'd have to look or listen very carefully to detect us.

From each of the troop carriers came six black-uniformed men. They were armed with new-looking submachine guns, and they wore armor and helmets with visors. The twelve of them gathered in a rough formation around Bill.

One of my goon escorts—I never did figure out which was Oberman and which was Manwaring—pulled me from the car and made me sit on the pavement. They stood over me with their submachine guns, trigger fingers ready. I looked up and saw the Ferris wheel, the same one Arie and I had spotted while searching the neighborhoods that day, the one that I had dreamt about.

"Bill," said Gary. "You heard what she said. They might have guards and they may be patrolling. I want your three best men to recon the park. No sounds. Quick and quiet. We're looking for any sign of activity. Don't engage unless fired on. Have them report ASAP."

Bill chose three of his Agency soldiers and sent them out.

Gary breathed in deeply and then leaned against the Crown Vic not too far from where I was seated on the ground. He seemed very content, almost relaxed.

"You've made the right decision, Alison," he said. "It's better this way."

"Yeah," I answered. "You're right."

"You know," he said, "I didn't think you'd come around this easily."

It was dark and I couldn't see his face clearly, but I knew he was smiling. I could hear it in his voice.

He said, "I thought things were going to have to get really ugly. With you. With Arie. Guess I was wrong."

I shrugged. "People can change."

We stayed in the parking lot for almost an hour. I sat on the pavement with my cuffed hands in my lap. The cold stars shone down. Then Bill got a report on his radio. He spoke in low tones, nodding.

"No patrols," he told Gary. "No sign of anything."

"Outstanding," Gary replied. "Get them back here."

Bill radioed the recon team.

"You know," said Gary, raising his voice a little. "If this thing goes as smoothly as I think it's going to, you're all getting steak and eggs on me for breakfast—and a three-day pass."

A murmur of appreciation rippled through the troops.

When the recon team returned, Gary said, "Okay, we're moving out. First squad, you'll be in the lead. Bill, Oberman, and Manwaring, you're with me with the prisoner in the middle. Second squad, bring up the rear."

The soldiers spread out and shuffled into a loose tactical formation.

Gary approached me and my goon escort. "You two," he said, pointing to Oberman and Manwaring, "remember what I said about her." He motioned to me.

"Don't worry, chief," one of them said. "She ain't going nowhere."

True.

"Let's move out," said Gary.

And so we stalked into the park. The lead soldiers darted from cover to cover, waving Gary and Bill along as each new passage was cleared and secure. They were well-trained—even I could tell. There were fifteen of them, and I barely heard any footsteps. They shuffled along with their weapons ready. They used hand signals and half the time I couldn't even see them in their black uniforms and armor.

I didn't actually know if any of Ruby's team was at the haunted house or even anywhere near. When last I'd spoken to Chase, I told them I was going to return to the ready room after I'd found the book I thought to be the key to Arie's coded notes. If they were leaving or going out on another mission, they would almost certainly have tried to get word to me, but Gary had been waiting for me when I got home. For all I knew, the team could be sound asleep in their bunks in the haunted house, or they could be miles away.

My plan would work either way.

Gary asked me for directions to the team hideout as we skulked through the amusement park. I told him exactly where to go, and Bill relayed the directions to the lead squad. We proceeded down the midway and past the Ferris wheel.

There were some nervous moments at the mouth of the tunnel, as the troops immediately realized it would be a perfect place for an ambush or trap.

Bill and Gary consulted at length as the troops crouched and knelt with their gun barrels pointed toward the tunnel.

"Let her go first," said Gary, pointing at me.

I walked through their ranks and into the tunnel, fifteen automatic weapons pointed at my back. When I made it to dim light at the far side of the tunnel, the soldiers followed me through and re-assembled in their formation.

Soon we stood at the front entrance to the haunted house. Everyone crouched in the darkness, weapons trained on the darkened building.

"Ah, the old hide-in-the-haunted-house trick, eh?" Gary whispered to me. "Very nice."

"That's their base," I said softly. "You have to go through the ride. It's a tunnel that winds around, but it's the only way in. It's like a maze in there and it's pitch-black. But there's sleeping quarters and a workroom inside. That's where they'll be."

"I don't like this," Bill whispered. "More tunnels?"

"Gary," I cut in. "I did my part. Your big tough goons can do the rest. Take me to Arie."

"No," said Gary. "Not yet. Alison, you're going in first."

"What? Why? What if there's shooting? I've done my part. We didn't say anything about me being your shield. Take me to Arie."

"You're a traitor," said Gary, his voice low. "I don't have to hold up my end of this deal. You're going to lead these men inside, or you won't see your son and you'll be executed for treason. What's it going to be?"

I said nothing. For all Gary's supposed power and troops, I found it almost disappointing that he was so easy to trick.

"That's what I thought," said Gary. "Now get over there."

I went to the front opening of the ride, where there was a gauntlet of turnstiles for the guests to pass through. The cars had all been removed, but there was a large archway where the ride began.

Interestingly, I'd never been through the front entrance. I'd always come through the back. I wouldn't have been able to find my way from the front entrance to the ready room or anywhere else.

But that didn't matter.

"First squad, follow her in," said Bill. "Second squad, cover the entrance."

Six of the men lined up in a sort of wedge behind me, ready to follow. Bill and Gary knelt a few yards behind me. The other six took up positions nearby, ready to fire on anyone who came out.

And so it was my time.

I stepped toward the turnstile. At the other rides, the turnstiles were locked. But I knew this one would not be locked. I knew that even with my cuffed hands I could push right through it.

Suddenly, I didn't feel ready. I wanted more time. A natural impulse given the situation, I suppose. But Arie was alive, and although I was sure his path would not be easy, I knew he would take care of himself. And for Ruby's team this was merely a courtesy for them—if they even needed it at all. Ruby's team? I didn't worry about them in the least.

I pushed the turnstile forward and it clunked once. I had promised myself I wouldn't hesitate or look back, but I couldn't help it. I looked back at Gary. It was nearly dawn again, and in the gathering light I could just make out his expression—satisfied, self-possessed, on the cusp of getting his way. I didn't know what kind of silly promotion or privileges he thought he was buying with his petty little attack on Ruby's team, but Gary knew, and you could tell by the look on his face that he could almost taste it.

When he saw me glance his way, however, his expression all at once changed. My true plan must have dawned on him. I'd accepted his offer of betrayal, but it wasn't Ruby I meant to betray.

"No," shouted Gary. "Stop her!"

I pushed the turnstile forward. It rolled forward again with a clunk.

Then came a cataclysmic, soul-shattering boom, and I was thrown back like a dry autumn leaf in the fiery wash of a jet engine.

And then the air was on fire.

And then I was on fire.

And then I was dead.

CHAPTER 26

For a long time, I heard angels singing. It might sound corny, but that's what came next. A chorus of harmonious notes that rang clearly and steadily without pause. Angels. And from behind my closed eyes, I saw white light.

But it wasn't angels. It was only a ringing in my ears. Or dreams. I was fading in and out of consciousness again, fading in and out of dreams. Dreams of Arie, dreams of Ruby and Chase and Woolly. There were dreams of fire, too.

Sometimes I thought I was alive and awake only to realize it was a dream, and at other times I wasn't sure about anything.

After what felt like a lifetime, I opened my eyes and knew I was somewhere real, and that I was alive.

I was in a bed. It was softer and warmer than any bed I'd slept in for as long as I could remember. The room had yellow walls and there was a window with white curtains that waved in a breeze. I sat up. My head pulsed with pain. My ribs, too. And my arms and legs.

"Hey, kiddo."

It was Chase. He sat in the corner, writing in a notebook. He smiled.

My ears rang continuously. I gaped open my mouth

to pop my ears, and the ringing subsided some. It would be a long time before it went away completely.

"How you feeling today?" Chase said. "Recognize me? Know who I am?"

"Of course I do. Why wouldn't I?"

"Let's just say you have good days and bad days," said Chase. He chuckled and set the notebook aside.

"I'm not dead?"

"No. Not anymore."

"What?"

"Well, you were dead when we pulled you out of the rubble. No pulse, no vitals. It was touch and go. We worked on you for quite a while. That's what happened to your ribs. CPR. Sorry. The rest is, apparently, self-inflicted."

"What do you mean? Where are we?" I asked.

"Safe house," Chase said. "We're safe." He stood up and walked to a bedside table where there was a pitcher of water and a tin cup. He filled the cup and handed it to me.

"There's tea, too, if you want that."

"My head hurts," I said, after drinking up the water. "And all the other parts of me."

"Yeah. It's a miracle you're alive," Chase said.

I touched my hand to my head and found it bandaged. My arms, too.

"What happened?"

"You don't remember anything?"

I shook my head.

"From what we can gather, you somehow got a bunch of goons to the front door of the HQ at the park and then tripped the C4 charges we wired to the turnstiles and front entrance."

That actually sounded like something I'd do.

I nodded a little.

But then a panicked feeling swept through me. "What about Ruby? And everyone else?"

"All safe," Chase said.

"Of course."

"You all right? This too much for ya?"

"How long have I been out?" I asked.

"Couple weeks," Chase said. "Well, you've been in and out. Like I said—good days and bad. Bad knock on the head, and then there's the matter of being, you know, somewhat dead. You're bound to have some memory gaps. I've actually told you all of this about twenty-five times over the past nine or ten days. Every now and then you're lucid. Other times you wake up and ask if you're in heaven, and so in case you're wondering about that, for the twenty-sixth time, no, this is not heaven."

"The goons?"

"Dead, most of them. A few might have pulled through. We patched them up and dropped them off at the infirmary. Gosford didn't make it."

When Chase said his name, all at once I remembered something else.

"Chase."

"Yeah?"

"Arie's alive."

"You found him?"

"No. Gary told me."

"And you believed him?"

"Yeah."

He came to the bed, wrapped his arms around me, and held me—though gingerly. "I'm so glad."

"I have to go find him," I said.

Chase nodded. "We'll find him. But you've got to recover, and there's something else to think about."

226

"What?"

Ruby stepped into the room. "I thought I heard y'all in here. How you doin' today, sweetie?"

"Ruby! Are you okay?" I said.

"Eh. I'm okay. Other than needin' to find a new HQ on account of you blew up the old one."

"You leveled half the park," Chase said. "We're beginning to notice a pattern here."

"I'm so sorry."

"Ah, don't worry about it," said Ruby. "It's at least half my doing. Guess I went a little crazy with the explosives. You doin' alright?"

"I think so. I don't know."

Ruby limped in and sat in the chair that Chase had vacated. "Wish you'da woken up a bit earlier. So we coulda had a bit more time."

"What do you mean?" I asked.

"That's what we gotta talk about," Chase said. "It's the new year. Past it. We need to take the serum."

"Okay. So? We have the clean serum, right? Don't tell me I destroyed that, too."

"No," said Ruby. "It wasn't at the park. We stashed it here. And we got enough for a hunerd people. But there's a problem."

"It's the wrong serum," Chase said. "Or maybe there is no clean serum. The serum we have has the same memory side effects."

"Glen and Carlos took it. Memories gone. They don't know any of us from a deep hole in the ground."

"No," I said. "I can't forget now that I know what I know. I've got to find Arie."

"You'll have to write it all down," Chase said. "That's what we've been doing. We're going to stagger the doses and try to explain everything to one another as we wake up."

I'd already written down everything about Arie I could think of. I didn't know where those journals were now, but even if I could get my hands on them, would it be enough?

"No," I said. "No. I can't. I just can't. I can't do it."

"We have to," Chase said. "You have to. You saw the graves. We're out of time."

"No," I repeated. "I was ready to die once. I'll do it again."

"What about Arie?" said Ruby.

Chase nodded.

"He's alive. Gary told me he is. He meant it and I believed him. And he told me I could see Arie if I showed him where the team's HQ was. I think Gary has recruited Arie into some program or group of his own. I know I could have seen him. So I know Arie is alive, and I'd give almost anything to see him, but I know he's smart and that he can take care of himself—and there are just certain things I won't do now, even if that means never seeing him again."

They argued with me. Tried to reason with me, but I refused to listen, and after going round and round until it was evening, they left. Later, Ruby brought me potatoes with a little very dry ham. I ate a bit, and when it was dark I fell asleep.

Then came a new series of vivid, nerve-wracking dreams. I dreamed I was with Gary in a house. I dreamed I was with Arie, but he didn't know who I was. I dreamed I was on the run from the Agency.

When I awoke it must have been after midnight. I sat in the bed, staring out at the night and the brilliantly black winter sky and its blazing star field.

Something tugged at the corners of my thoughts.

Something I'd forgotten to do? Something I'd forgotten to say? Or was it something someone had said to me?

I stood up, and before I knew it, I was limping around the house to find Chase's bedroom. I would have shaken him awake, but apparently I'd already woken him up by shambling through the house. I stood in the open doorway of his room. In the starlight I saw him sitting up in his bed.

"Al? That you?" he said in the dark.

"What if there is no serum?" I said.

"What are you talking about?" Chase asked. "Are you okay? Come over here and sit down. Do you know where you are?"

"Yes, I'm fine," I said, crossing the room. I sat on the bed with him. "I'm awake. I'm lucid. I know we're not in heaven. Okay? Chase, what if there's no serum at all? I mean what if the so-called serum does nothing else but erase our memories?"

"Sure," he said, "I've thought of that, heard rumors." He sounded perplexed. "But it's pretty risky to stake your life on rumors generated by a bunch of half-starved people who can't remember anything from longer ago than a year, don't you think?" Then through a big yawn, he added, "Why are you awake? What's this about?"

"It's something Gary said," I told him. "He threatened to have my memory wiped. Like it was a punishment. Like it was something they could do at any time—not a side effect of the serum, but something the Agency did to keep us in line."

He was quiet for a moment. Then he said, "Still risky, Al. Still really risky."

He was right, of course. It'd be betting my life on a hunch and rumors. I considered everything that had happened in the past year, and before that, and all that I wanted to do next. I wanted to find Arie, and I wanted to be together with him again. But the Agency was obviously keeping secrets—the most deep and damaging sort of secrets—and I couldn't give in to them for another year, or sell myself out in any other way, even if the reward was a reunion with Arie. I didn't want that and neither would he.

And what world was I living in, if not a world of risks and high stakes? We almost died—the whole human race. I'd already overcome incredible odds just to sit there in the silvery darkness with Chase. Yes, I was afraid to die, but I'd tried it once, and it'd worked out all right. I would not keep living the Agency's way—one life at a time, the ghost of a ghost.

"Chase, I remember now. I remember how we ended up at the haunted house. Gary had me cornered. It was checkmate. I knew I couldn't betray you and Ruby, and I was out of moves. It was weird. As soon as I realized I'd have to trip those explosives, I saw everything with incredible clarity. And I knew if I could just take Gary out of the game, you guys and Arie would be okay. You'd carry on. Even if it meant taking myself out. It was like I saw the whole game board for the first time. Clearly. And I feel like I'm seeing things clearly now. I'm telling you: there is no serum. It's all a game."

In the dark I saw him raise a hand. "But you saw the—"

"—graves," I said. "I know. We saw the bones. I believe there was a virus. Of course there was. But we survived. I think that's what happened. We're immune, or our immune systems adapted. I don't know. All I know is I'm not playing by their rules anymore, Chase. Live or die. I'm done. I'm never going to take it."

"Me neither," said Ruby. "Me neither, goddamit."

She'd been standing in the doorway. It made me jump.

"She's real sneaky," said Chase.

"When I need ta be," said Ruby with a laugh.

"So—what?" said Chase. "We're having a meeting about this? Now? In my room?"

"Should we wake up Woolly?" I said.

"You can try," said Ruby.

"He sleeps like the dead," said Chase. He fumbled at the side table by the bed and lit a candle.

"There's no convincing either of you?" he said.

"No," we said in unison.

"Well, I never intended to take it," said Chase. "But I wasn't going to tell you that." He laughed and then sleepily rubbed his face.

"I got a bottle of Dewars," said Ruby. "Let me run and get it. Get the cups and wake up ole Woolly. Might as well have a drink. We may not have much longer on this old earth."

CHAPTER 27

Carlos and Glen were gone. They'd never been much more than hired hands to Ruby, and I guess she saw no further need to put them at risk—especially now that their memories had been erased. And they weren't much of a threat to Ruby's operation anymore, so Chase told them as much as they needed to know and led them blindfolded to the Taurus. He said he dropped them off just outside the Zone boundary, where they'd hopefully be recovered by a patrol and reunited with their families.

Woolly was different. He was an essential member of the team, and, frankly, we all loved him.

At first, we were devastated when he told us that he'd decided to take the serum.

"I'll even out the odds," he explained after we'd toasted with our tin cups of Dewars. "If you three fall over and die, I'll be around to carry on. I'm not giving up. If what Alison says is true—or rather if what Gary told Alison is true—I'll read my notebooks and yours, and then fall into my old wicked ways and pick up somewhere close to where we all left off. We have to even out these odds. We have to guarantee that somebody lives through this. In fact, one of you three should do what I'm doing. Then we guarantee that two of us live. You guys aren't thinking this through."

But we were as steadfast as he was—I was convinced the serum was just a game, and even though Woolly's arguments made perfect logical sense, I would never willingly take the serum again.

However, when I thought about it too much, it did feel like an extraordinary gamble. Sometimes the fear wrapped around me like a thick wet blanket. I had panic attacks, didn't sleep well.

But we kept our agreement, our joint decision to die—maybe. Woolly would die for sure, but only his identity, and he'd have his notebooks and ours to back him up. The rest of us might also die but if we lived, we'd live intact, with a year of memories, and we'd re-train Woolly. It was like some kind of open-ended suicide pact.

Arie had told me once about an experiment he'd read about in a magazine. It began with laboratory monkeys kept in cages, and in every cage researchers placed a toy—a doll or rubber ball or something. Naturally, the monkeys wanted to touch the toys, but when they did, the researchers subjected them to a harsh and startling blast of air. And so the monkeys quickly learned that the toys were not to be touched under any circumstances. Next, the researchers placed a second group of monkeys into the cages. These new arrivals wanted to touch the toys, too, but the original group prevented them from doing so—saving the new monkeys from the unpleasant stimulus. Then, the original monkeys were replaced with a third group of monkeys. The only monkeys to have ever been subjected to the harsh air blasts were now gone, but again, the new monkeys were curious about the toys. The monkeys in the second group intervened, however, even though they'd never been subjected to the negative stimulus. The researchers wouldn't and didn't subject the monkeys to any more blasts of air, but even so, none of the monkeys would touch the toys, based solely on the passed-along knowledge of the monkeys from the first group, who'd known about the air blasts firsthand—monkeys which were now gone.

I was placing my bet that we were like that third group of monkeys, continuing to take the treatment, giving up our very identities, and doing so based on some long-ago threat that probably no longer existed and maybe was never really there in the first place.

How does one characterize luck? My life in the Zone had been rather miserable at times—scraping by without hope of a better life, going to bed hungry, living in fear. But I had been lucky, luckier than a person had a right to expect in an entire lifetime. I had survived the pandemic, for one thing, which, judging from just that one mass grave site, was an astronomical stroke of fortune. And I had Arie. Surely other survivors could not have been so lucky. Arie and I had survived for who knew how many years without the benefit of our memories—how much luck had that required? And then, just over the last few months, I'd been shot at and driven off a cliff and blown up by C4 explosives.

So, why me? Why had I survived when others hadn't? Why had I been adopted into a group that seemed poised to free a population of abject refugees from an unending annual cycle of misery? It certainly wasn't because I had a survival instinct or was particularly smart or brave. There was nothing special about me that would make me more likely to survive than anyone else. It had all come down to luck.

Outside, the birds were chirping. Spring was coming. The days were warm but it turned bitterly cold at night, and in the morning hoarfrost sometimes covered the trees and winter-dead grass.

It had taken a while for me to get well enough to move around much. In addition to a periodic fogginess of mind and unsteadiness of my balance, the explosive blast at the haunted house had left me with lots of lacerations and burns. My ankle and knee were sore and stiff, and there were the cracked ribs Chase had given me in the process of bringing me back from the dead. But after a few weeks, I was able to walk to join the others for meals.

"Still alive, I see," Chase would say to me when I appeared at breakfast.

"Have we met?" I'd reply. "I'm not sure I recall."

But it was an odd time for all of us, even given the bizarre turns we'd already taken together.

After taking the serum, Woolly slept for almost three whole days. He'd wake up once or twice a day, long enough only to sip a bit of water or broth or tea, and he didn't forget all at once. On the morning of the second day, he opened his eyes and said he was thirsty. I gave him a tin cup of water, and after he drank it, he handed it to me and said, "Thanks, Al."

But the following day at sundown, Woolly came out of his room with a look on his face that told us he was utterly lost. We knew then that the serum had taken its course and that he'd no longer remember us.

Ruby greeted him by wrapping her arm around him.

"I know you probably feel really outta sorts right now," she said lovingly, "but we're gonna explain everything to ya. You can ask us any questions you like. We'll answer."

He regarded her with more than token suspicion.

"My name's Ruby. That there's Alison, and he's Chase. We're your friends."

"Hello," he said weakly.

We waved.

"What would you like to know?" asked Chase, smiling sadly at his friend, his chess partner.

"Well," said Woolly in his polite but deliberate way, "for starters, who am I? I can't seem to remember my name."

"Oh, right," said Ruby. "I forgot ya'd forget because normally you don't forget nothin'. Anyhow, your name's William. We call ya Woolly, on account of your woolly hair and your big beard, see. And you're one 'a the smartest fellas we ever met."

Ruby ushered him to a chair in the living room.

Woolly nodded slowly as we told him about the pandemic and the serum. The next day we explained the Agency and the Zones and the events of the entire last year. I told him about Arie and Gracie. Chase told him about Carlos and Glen. And there were others.

Woolly read and re-read the notebooks he'd written, sometimes staring incredulously at his own handwriting.

"It's hard to take in," said Woolly. "It's hard to believe."

"Yah," said Ruby. "It's too bad you had to take the serum. It was your idea, an' it was a smart one, but it's still too damn bad."

Ruby had stories of people who'd been on the team but had been captured and killed—stories I'd never heard.

We told Woolly everything we knew, everything we could think of. It seemed to rush out of us, almost as though we couldn't tell him fast enough, maybe because we honestly didn't know how much time we had.

Days passed by. We sat around for hours talking as we drank tea or took walks after sunset—all the while

236

waiting day by day for the virus to emerge, to take effect.

Chase kept us all on a watch schedule, but we never saw a sign of the Agency.

"They're rebuilding, planning," theorized Chase one night as he relived me on guard duty. "A lot of what they knew about us probably died with Gosford and his pals. Whoever replaced them will resume their search for us at some point, but with the end of the year serum treatment and the security breaches and the casualties, they won't be ready to move on us again for a while."

And so even though those days were little more than a tedious group death-watch, there was laughter and overall it was a very good time. We played chess and wrote in our journals and in the evenings we sat at the fireplace and speculated about where we might be in another year or two.

God, how precious those memories became.

The days grew longer. It was like a new sun was rising—not the dreary depressed sun of winter, but the bright energetic sun of spring. It was the beginning of March and none of us had shown any sign of illness. In fact, we seemed to become healthier with each passing day. The rations stockpiled at the safe house were not luxurious, and at times they were somewhat vile—stale flour and grains, canned foods that had exceeded their optimal shelf life, and dried meats and fruits that were barely more palatable than old gym shoes. But something about being apart from the Agency and its enforced misery revived us.

Then, one morning as the four of us shared a breakfast of cracked wheat and blackstrap molasses, I made my announcement.

"I'm leaving," I said.

Chase looked up abruptly.

"Whaddya mean?" asked Ruby.

"We're alive," I said. "We've survived. The serum is a sham. I have to go tell the others."

"What others?" asked Woolly.

"Everyone," I said. "But first, I've got to find my son. He's alive. The Agency knows where he is. I can't wait another day. If we were going to die, it would have happened by now. I'm well enough to travel. I have to go."

"Where you gonna start?" asked Chase. "What's your plan?"

I didn't know. Not for certain. I had to go back to the Zone that Gary supervised to pick up Arie's trail, but what was I going to do then? Break into the depot? The infirmary?

Ruby dropped her spoon into her bowl. "Well, y'ain't goin' alone, if that's what you're tryna say."

It was exactly how I'd hoped she'd respond, but still I replied, "You don't have to come with me. You could head south, like you've talked about. Find out what's going on out in the world. This is something I need to do and it doesn't have to involve you."

"The hell's that s'posed to mean?" clucked Ruby. She turned to Chase. "Chay, what's she talking about?"

Chase shrugged. Ruby turned back to me.

"That was our bargain wasn't it? The trade for you drivin' the truck? We got what we wanted—we don't gotta take the serum no more. Now let's get that smarty-pants son 'a yours and burn them lying bastards to the ground. Ain't we still all in this together?"

"Yeah, Al," said Chase. "Don't be dramatic. Of course we're coming with you. If you're ready to start again, then we are, too. Woolly'll come, won'tcha?"

"Well, not so fast," said Woolly without looking up

from his bowl. "I don't fully know what I'm getting myself into here. I don't know any of you very well, and I don't even know if anything you're saying is true or reasonable or valid. I hope you understand. It would be exceedingly reckless of me to get involved in what sounds like some very dangerous activity."

We all stared at him. He ate a spoonful of his porridge.

"Thing is," he went on. "I don't have anything else to do. I've got literally nothing else planned. Ever. So. I'm in."

"Psh," exhaled Chase. "Some things don't change, I guess."

I never could get Ruby or Chase to explicitly calculate the odds that we'd be killed or captured by going back, and even though we didn't talk much about the prospect of being dosed again and having our minds swept clean once more, we'd already proven that the Agency wasn't strong enough to keep us apart. We were ready to prove it again.

As we prepared our gear for a trip back, a knot of dread sometimes formed in my stomach. We were going back to the Zone, back to that bleakness, that hellscape of dark, ramshackle neighborhoods populated by blank stares and ghosts. Back to the streets patrolled by skulking goons and hulking black war machines. Back to that prison of the mind that some person or group had tried to hold us in.

This time, though, it would be different. Not only were we going together as a team, but this time we were heavily armed. With rifles and weapons, yes, but also with something much more powerful—this time we had our memories. We had what the Agency desperately did not want us to have—ourselves.

Get Book Two

Among These Bones continues in
When It's No Longer Night.

Available now at:
www.amazon.com/dp/B07PN2R12L

To be notified of new releases,
sign up for Amanda's newsletter
on her website:

www.amandaluzzader.com

Need more Amanda Luzzader?
Pick up thirteen deeply creepy short
horror stories in
CREEP FACTOR.

Available now at:
www.amazon.com/dp/B07J3X1CM5

To be notified of new releases,
sign up for Amanda's newsletter
on her website:

www.amandaluzzader.com

Acknowledgments

Without Chadd VanZanten, this book would not have been possible. I still remember standing in his kitchen while he tried to convince me that the short story I had written should be expanded into a novel. It was only with his insistence and encouragement that I began this endeavor. Chadd helped me by co-writing an earlier version of this book and then by acting as editor and copywriter. He is a writing genius. I'd be thrilled to have even one-tenth of his talent. Chadd is my brilliant editor, forever friend, confidante, and now passionate lover and husband. I admire him endlessly.

I also owe a debt of gratitude to my writing group. Learning about writing would not have been nearly so much fun without them. Thanks especially to our fearless leader, Tim Keller. To E.B. Wheeler, Tim "Turbo" Tarbet, Britney Johnson, Felicia Rose, Eric Bishop, Sherrie Lynn Clarke (SLC), Jeremy Gohier, Casey Gasper, Lori Johnson Parker, Dustin Earl, Jeff Ricks, Jeff Bateman, Robyn Buttars, Emily Olsen, Lora Ann Stead, Arielle Hadfield, Shauna Leavitt, Neil Dabb, Isaac and Aaron Timm, Lynne Allen, and Wally Pride—thank you for your advice, insight, and help, but most importantly for making me laugh until my eyes watered over cherry pie at Village Inn or sweet potato fries at Angie's. I'm glad that we agree that Solo shot first and that Picard is better than Kirk. Thank you for indulging my obsession with *Downton Abbey* and *How I Met Your Mother*. These are important matters.

Thank you to my family. To my children, Hudson and Dawson, who are so patient with the extra time I spend writing and make super creative and thoughtful suggestions: you are both brilliant. I am so lucky to be your mother.

To my sister Jennifer, I think I would have given up multiple times if it hadn't been for your encouragement. You believed in me more than I believed in myself. I am so thankful. Thank you for your psychiatric help, brainstorming with me, and motivating me.

Thank you, Melissa, book expert of our family. Thank you for giving me good books to read, for sharing your knowledge of what makes for interesting and compelling plots, and for being my friend. I'm sad you're moving. Let's hang out.

Finally, to my parents, Bob and Barbra. If I have any talent for writing, I believe it comes from you. My mother has a gift for words and language, and my father has a gift for thinking outside the box and coming up with solutions. Both have proven that they will always be there to help.

To everyone mentioned above—I love you! It is all of you who make life worth living and worth writing about. I will never forget you.

About the author

Amanda Luzzader writes up market science fiction and horror, and she is a self-described 'fraidy cat. Things she will run away from include (but are not limited to): mice, snakes, spiders, bits of string and litter that resemble spiders, most members of the insect kingdom, and (most especially) bats. Bats are the worst. But Amanda is first and primarily a mother to two energetic and intelligent sons, and this role inspires and informs her writing, which frequently involves mothers and women as main characters. As Amanda likes to say, "Moms are people, too."

Amanda has worked as a technical writer and a professional editor and is currently employed as a grant writer for a Utah nonprofit organization. She is a devout cat person.

www.amandaluzzader.com

Made in the USA
Middletown, DE
17 September 2019